THE SHADOW
WHISTLER

THE SHADOW
WHISTLER

ROYCE WALKER

iUniverse LLC
Bloomington

THE SHADOW WHISTLER

iUniverse books may be ordered through booksellers or by contacting:

iUniverse LLC
1663 Liberty Drive
Bloomington, IN 47403
www.iuniverse.com
1-800-Authors (1-800-288-4677)

ISBN: 978-1-4917-3215-1 (sc)
ISBN: 978-1-4917-3216-8 (hc)
ISBN: 978-1-4917-3214-4 (e)

Library of Congress Control Number: 2014909001

Printed in the United States of America.

iUniverse rev. date: 06/18/14

CONTENTS

PART ONE

THE HOLE

THE FIGURE PERCHED QUIETLY on the nearby riverbank, watching the road leading to the one-lane car tunnel. The figure was tolerant of the cold air, the mist of his breath flittering in front of his nose as he breathed in and out. His eyes were tired but were aggressively alert, the way an old field hand looked on the afternoon of the first day of harvest. Everything was important.

The weather was overcast, almost feeling like snow but not quite there. The day felt like it was time in suspense—no sound, no movement, only the foggy breath coming from the figure on the riverbank.

The figure was all gray. It seemed to be wearing a threadbare pair of overalls with a hood pulled up over his head. It fit his body closely, as if it had been tailored to prevent being snagged on brush and prickly bushes as he ran through the woods. From across the field, it looked like maybe he was a workman or a farmer or a ghost.

Far down the road, a small dot along the highway grew larger as it approached—a car. It wasn't driving too fast, perhaps as fast as a horse could gallop. The figure watched it, and spoke to itself.

Bunny Man see them coming for the hole.

The car grew in size until it almost grew past the width of the short, one-lane tunnel beneath the railroad tracks, and then, in a quiet whoosh, it passed through and made its way along the field by the riverbank.

Bunny Man gonna eat their guts.

The figure was suddenly gone, and the space where he had been standing was still. The birds, which had been feeding in the field, had fled.

Bunny Man gonna do some work.

The car made its way farther down the road and then pulled to the side and stopped along the bank.

Three people got out of the car and stood along the roadside, two

3

young men and a young woman. They laughed. The men began chasing the woman around the car, the woman laughing and making jokes. Finally, they all collided and began wrestling with their clothes.

Bunny Man gonna eat their guts.

The woman gasped out of delight as her skin was exposed to the cold air; the men pulled on her clothes, and she laughed. She pulled on their clothes, and they laughed too.

The gray figure was suddenly closer to them, standing at an odd angle to the car, just out of their field of vision.

The backs of the two men were to the gray figure, and as he stepped forward, more and more quickly, the figure could hear their short, quick breaths. The girl's mouth moved between the two men, while the men fondled her breasts and feverishly worked their hands under her skirt.

The girl laughed.

Bunny Man gonna eat.

The girl's eyes looked far away, and then as she was distracted for just a moment, she saw the gray shape staring at her. Her eyes grew as large as her face, and she panicked

Bunny Man gonna get his food.

The figure ripped the head of the first man sideways, almost separating it from the shoulders. The second man was caught by surprise, and as he turned sharply to face the figure, the figure moved around him and grabbed both his arms from behind, jerking them violently and back. Two loud snaps were heard by the girl as she watched the man collapse.

In a quick moment, the girl found herself stunned and sprawled out from the force of a blow she didn't remember receiving. She was unable to breathe.

The figure was gone. The girl tried to prop herself up against the side of the car, her skirt torn and sopped with blood from her chest. Her face was quickly growing pale.

She struggled to come to full consciousness, her head lifting slightly, her eyes peering off into the distant field. She tried hard to focus. She could see the figure pulling one of the men behind him by the ankle and then lifting him up and steadying the man upright.

Then she saw the figure reach up and pull down on the man's chest. The man stayed standing, his head bobbing, but quickly fell flat onto the dirt.

As her vision went dark, the girl slipped sideways, and her face hit the cold soil.

THE FARMER

The farmer was on his tractor, slowly driving past the fence line along the boundary of his property. He had seen the car there for a few hours and thought it might be hunters looking for pheasants or bird-watchers or a traveling salesman sleeping off a long trip on a back road. He just wanted to take a look.

The farmer saw something lying on the ground but couldn't tell what it was.

He drove farther along the fence and then stopped and stood, his hand up over his eyes as he tried to filter out some of the midday glare.

He could just make out the shape of a body on the bank, maybe two. *Were they sleeping?* he wondered.

He sat back down and pressed on the gas harder; the tractor picked up a little more speed.

The farmer made his way along the frontage road that led to the highway and was just about to turn when he saw a piece of fabric hanging from the barbed wire fence. He didn't pay it any attention until he was almost past it, when he realized it was part of an animal hanging there.

A limb, some guts, some skin, and ... a foot—a human foot. And part of a head.

It was dried out, almost like the fluids had been sucked out of it and left to freeze overnight. Parts of the skin lifted in the light wind, like the mummified carcass of a coyote shot for killing chickens or livestock. It was hanging there like it had been left as a warning to other coyotes to stay away.

It didn't smell. It didn't look angry. It just was.

Off in the distance—down the road, across the highway, and in a thicket by the one-lane tunnel—the gray man watched, and then he was gone.

This Bunny Man's hole.
This my hole.
This been my hole; this gonna be my hole.
This gonna feed me and keep me warm.
This Bunny Man's hole.

THE LAND SELLER

T HE FOR SALE SIGN had only been up a few days when a real estate
developer made an offer on the land. It was eighty-one acres
bisected by the railroad tracks, with a highway running diagonally across
the land. It was part of a bigger parcel that was going to be kept for crops.
The buyer wanted to survey the property with the seller just to clear up
any questions.

The two drove out to the property. It was a mild afternoon, with
bright sidelight for that time of year. Out in the field across the highway
they saw the farmer on his tractor turning over soil.

The buyer walked out into the parcel several hundred yards, while
the seller stayed on the road. The seller was an old man. He felt bad about
having to sell off a portion of the land his family had owned since the
Civil War, but he had to do it. He needed the money.

The buyer had a camera with him, and he took several pictures of the
field, the railroad track running back into the woods, and the trees along
the riverfront bank. He stopped for a moment, looking toward the tunnel
that ran under the railroad, and then he meandered back.

"That's quite a spread," the buyer said. "It looks stable. I think we
can use it. But I just wondered—how many easements do you have for
this piece of land?"

The seller looked back at the farmer on his tractor and pointed. "Just
him. Why?"

The buyer pointed back to the woods along the riverfront bank. "I
just thought I saw a guy digging along the bank over there and figured
maybe there might be a house back there."

"Nope, no houses back there. Just woods, a few deer trails. Kids used
to come out here at night and make campfires and drink beer, though.
No one else is ever out here."

The seller nodded, looked again toward the spot where he had seen

9

the gray figure, and then turned back and headed toward the car. As he walked away, he caught a glimpse out of the corner of his eye of a gray streak that seemed to move suddenly. He turned again and stopped, focusing his attention on the woods.

"There," he said to the seller. He raised his arm and pointed. "Is that a man standing there?"

The seller turned and looked as well, stopping for a moment. There did appear to be something there, but as he squinted, the shadow faded in the light.

He shook his head and then said, "Must be a deer. They're out there—big ones too. A few years back my nephew got himself a big buck, must have been a nine pointer, I think."

Bunny Man gonna keep this hole.

Bunny Man gonna keep this hole forever.

THE TRAVELING SALESMAN

THE TRAVELING SALESMAN WAS late getting home. The rain, the bad roads, and that long call in town had kept him from getting back in time for dinner.

The rain had stopped but the road was still wet, so he drove cautiously along the highway. He'd seen more than a few deer along the road; it was rutting season, and he didn't want to crash.

He saw the big black dot up ahead—the one-lane tunnel. It looked like a dot at night. The face of the tunnel itself was white, but the tunnel had no lights inside or on the other side of it, so it always looked like a dot.

The salesman saw a train on the tracks heading along the line, going at about the same pace, and he wondered if he was going to make it through the tunnel before it crossed overhead.

He remembered a rhyme his grandmother had taught him out on the farm when he was a boy, on the farm near where he was now, which went something like, "When the train and the tunnel are crossed at the same time, the gray man will pop out of his hole."

He never really knew what that meant.

The train began to pick up speed, so he did too. Then he saw the engineer in the window of the locomotive look his way and heard a toot of the whistle. The black dot grew closer.

The salesman eased off the accelerator and let the car coast through the short tunnel. With the window rolled down, he could hear the sound of his engine, and he listened for noises. He didn't hear a thing.

He passed through the tunnel and turned to look at where the train was. It was gone into the woods. As he turned back toward the road, two giant red eyes stared back at him from the darkness ahead.

He slammed on the brakes, and the car skidded sideways, almost heading into the ditch along the frontage road. He screamed as he turned the wheel the other way, causing the car to cross the opposite direction into the field, where it came to an abrupt stop.

He sat there for a moment, trembling. There were voices coming from the radio … an evening radio show, the light of the radio casting itself into the car.

The man looked around, almost afraid to get out, but then he steadied himself, opened the door, and stepped out.

Bunny Man don't like no noise.

Bunny Man don't like no cars.

Bunny Man own that hole.

The salesman stood on the running board and looked around. He came to his senses when another car passed through the tunnel and drove up past him. It stopped.

The driver rolled down his window and said in a loud voice, "Hey, mister, you stuck?"

"Nah, just driving like a dickless bastard. Thanks, though."

"Sure 'nough." The driver sped away.

Bunny Man got red eyes.

Bunny Man know that train.

Bunny Man gonna find that nest.

The man stepped off the running board, slipped behind the wheel, and put the car in reverse gear. The wheels spun a bit, but the car finally backed onto the highway. Feeling better, the salesman shifted into drive and sped off. As he drove away, he looked in the rearview mirror and saw a figure standing on the road where he had just been.

Two giant red eyes burned brightly in the night, running right behind his car. There was a flash of rotten teeth under them—big teeth, and long.

He stepped hard on the accelerator and moved quickly away, now more scared than ever. His house was just up ahead. As he looked for the porch lights, he noticed an old man sitting in a rocking chair on the porch of the farmhouse across the highway. The man stood and looked at the salesman as he drove past, gesturing and seemingly shouting at him.

Bunny Man own that hole.

THE GHOST

T HE KIDS PARKED ALONG the bank and walked into the woods. They brought with them a transistor radio, some matches to start a fire, and the beer.

The group gathered some wood while some of the others dug out the pit within the circle of rocks they had placed there the last time. They piled the wood up, added some tinder underneath, and struck the match.

The fire slowly caught and then roared to life.

The kids sat on logs and the ground around the warm fire, drinking beer and laughing as they sang along with the music.

Then one kid said he had a scary story to tell them.

"It's about the ghost of the Gray Man," he began. "He lives here. This was his land. My grandfather told me the story. There used to be an insane asylum out here during the Civil War filled with war criminals and murderers. This guy bought a house on the property in 1927 and eventually went crazy and killed his family with a metal pipe, and they locked him up there and never let him out. No one saw him except when they put food through the door into his cell. They said he had turned gray from never having seen the sun."

The other kids laughed.

But the boy continued his story. "Then, one night, on a night like this one, there was a big storm. The storm knocked over a huge tree by the building, and it broke down the wall. The Gray Man escaped, and he's been hunting the families of the people who threw him in there ever since."

The kids laughed even louder and continued to drink their beer.

"They tracked him and found a giant hole in the ground where they discovered pieces of animals that had been torn apart—like ripped apart with teeth. Something had been sleeping there during the day and roaming the land at night looking for people to kill. Lots of people have disappeared here without a trace.

"They never found Gray Man. But down the road from here another family was killed—mutilated. They were ripped open and their insides thrown around the room, their hearts torn from their chests and partially eaten. Turns out, the man was the brother of the prosecutor who had sent the Gray Man to jail.

"The Gray Man killed him, his wife, their three kids, and even their dog—ripped the dog's head off and threw it in the fireplace. The whole house smelled like roast dog when they found the bodies. You don't even want to know what he did to the wife—opened her up and slept in her guts. My grandpa says the investigators threw up when they went inside. Blood was everywhere!"

The boy telling the story shouted, and everyone else screamed and then laughed.

They all drank, and the couples began kissing and going off away from the fire. The smell of pot filled the air.

Bunny Man don't like no smell.

Bunny Man gonna eat their guts.

Bunny Man gonna get warm.

THE SHERIFF

THE SHERIFF HAD A book he kept locked in his desk drawer. He never showed anyone what was in its pages.

Inside, he kept a collection of newspaper articles and Teletype messages he'd been gathering for more than thirty years. There were some photographs as well, along with some coroners' reports, automobile accident reports, and autopsy notes. Everything inside that book was about something he couldn't explain.

He had long suspected that there was something unusual going on out there along the railroad track, the portion that passed through the farm belt by the river. He had thought for a long time that he might have a serial killer operating in the area and that bodies were being dumped there, brought from some other place. Most of the people went unidentified for a long time, and all of them were almost unrecognizable when their families or friends finally went to the morgue to view the bodies.

The sheriff had thought it was likely a traveling salesman or a truck driver, someone who frequented the area but was always in transit, almost never around long enough to attract any suspicion. When people aren't feeling threatened, they oftentimes don't pay any attention—that was one thing he had learned after so many years of being a deputy, then a fireman, and, finally, the sheriff.

He did have a serial killer out there. He just couldn't figure out what kind of serial killer.

He knew the stories. He himself had grown up playing along that stretch of track, swimming in the river, dodging trains, and hunting squirrels, and he had seen the Gray Man. He knew he was out there. He'd seen him while pheasant hunting and while surveying some land out there along the greenbelt. But every time he went looking for him, there was no sign except torn-up animal flesh and bits of bone. There were never any footprints, never any other clues.

He just couldn't think of a way to catch him.

The sheriff had pored over the material in his book in private and had often added bits and pieces to the book even if the material wasn't really part of the collection. He just had feelings at times that there was more to this than he knew.

Too many bodies … and too many full moons and cold mornings with strange things going on out there.

He couldn't explain it. But there was one thing he knew: every one of those people who had died had driven through the railway tunnel, from the township side into the farm belt when there was a train coming along. *That* he was certain of.

There was something out there bent on murder. How it did it or why, he didn't know.

THE MORTICIAN

T HE MORTICIAN HAD BEEN hired by the county to replace the medical examiner but hadn't yet taken the office, so he was still working at the local mortuary. He wasn't sure he wanted the new job. Three medical examiners had quit in the past ten years.

Stress.

For a small town on the fringes of the countryside, there sure did seem to be a lot of strange deaths. They couldn't really call them murders. It was more like they were freak deaths … people dropped into hay-baling machines … people sucked into industrial washing machines … people strangled by their own neckties while watching a cake being mixed in a kitchen appliance. It was all almost like silent retribution.

And then there were the real killings too. There were the people who looked like they'd been gutted by an animal. Sometimes bodies appeared to have been eaten from the inside out. Aside from the challenges of physical restoration, making sense of how they were killed was even more challenging. It wasn't part of the job, but it was becoming part of the routine.

As for his craft, the mortician was reaching the limits of his skill. There were only so many ways a mortician could make a mutilated body look normal. Inflating and stuffing plastic bags inside the chest cavity, painting on skin, even sculpting some skin out of plaster and airbrushing it—all these things had their limits. Some things simply couldn't be hidden.

Replacing ripped limbs was tougher, because they had to look natural when covered in clothing. And missing heads were impossible to cope with no matter what.

The mortician had spent several years as an army corpsman in Eastern Europe. During his time overseas, he had worked at many rural care stations and hospice houses and had seen almost every compression and trauma injury known to mankind. Some were old-school injuries from when manual labor was truly a way of surviving. But he'd also seen bodies ripped apart by bombs, bodies ripped apart by machines, bodies ripped apart by Muslims, and bodies drawn and quartered by teams of horses as punishment for adultery.

He'd even seen a man cooked from the inside out, his body filled with fuel oil and lit on both ends at once. Eventually, the gas inside the body would expand and create an air pocket, and then, with a *whomp*, the body would likely come apart in one big pop. The outside skin would look normal, but the inside would look like it had been charred. The corpsmen called it the ray-gun effect, like it came from outer space or something.

There were many regions of the world where the laws of ancient folklore still ruled. The tearing out of tongues and the gouging out of eyes were fairly common. The lopping off of hands for theft and the crushing of bones were widespread. The mortician had even seen a man crucified in western China, left on a tree for days. Who knows how long he had lived before he finally expired. The organs of the body had eventually balled themselves into a mass and caused the stomach to hang down like a laundry bag until someone had taken a sword and slashed it open, spilling everything down onto the ground for the dogs and the crows.

But the kinds of things he was seeing here were … well, different. It was like a combination of things together—an animal, a man, a piece of machinery. He couldn't tell which it was.

When the three bodies from the riverbank highway were brought in, he knew there was something out there that must have had another element to it. This was something new, something he'd never seen. The man's chest had been ripped open like the top of a shipping box, as if something had reached around him from behind, split him down the middle, and opened him up. His ribs were snapped back, exposing the chest like a rack of spare ribs turned inside out.

The mortician called a friend from the army who had specialized in cataloging battlefield injuries and asked about the power needed to break open a man's ribcage.

"Never seen it done," the friend admitted. "Not even getting hit with a rocket from behind would do that. You'd have to keep the victim upright and pull equally hard on both sides by ripping through the skin first and then pushing like hell from behind to make them break off. Don't see how it could be possible. Maybe with a set of chains or even a big knife you could split the ribcage. But what for?"

The mortician said he didn't know either.

THE BUS DRIVER

THE BUS DRIVER DROVE a service line that ran parallel to the old highway along the riverbank. Sometimes he'd be out getting his bus to the first pickup early in the morning, sometimes as late as eleven o'clock at night. He sat way up high. The bus was a new one, with all the features to make him comfortable. It had high-powered headlights and even a set of side spotlights for courtesy when people were unloading and trying to find their bags in the side hatch.

He liked that early morning trip. During certain times of the year, the morning light would come at such an odd angle that everything looked like it was painted in oil—texture, contrast, detail. He was an amateur painter himself and painted in his time off between the long trips he'd drive.

He'd seen deer in the fields along the railroad, sometimes a bear, sometimes a bobcat. Lots of birds—pheasant and some turkeys too. He could see their misty breath with that funny morning sidelight coming across the field. He'd often thought of trying to paint it but knew he'd never do it justice.

He'd also seen something else out there. It looked almost like a big dog. It must have been an old dog, because it was all gray and was often sitting on its haunches in the middle of the field, with heavy breath, panting.

But the big dog was incredibly fast. Usually by the time the bus driver was close enough to the field to get a really good look, it was already gone.

The bus driver could almost make out its head and overall shape, and then he would pass behind a small slope on the riverbank for a second before turning away from the railroad. There was a tunnel up there, too small for the bus to pass through comfortably, although the bus driver had gone out there once with a measuring tape and checked it. He'd have maybe ten inches to spare all the way around, both top and sides.

In his younger days driving trucks, he'd never have given it a second thought, but with a new roadliner bus, he didn't want to risk it.

The bus driver had gotten to know the local coal train engineer, and sometimes in the mornings there'd be a load of coal coming in along the same track. They'd wave, and the bus driver would check his speed by the train. The train could only go fifty-two miles per hour under a full load and on a flat trail. He'd pace the train and then close his eyes just for a moment before checking the speedometer. This one had hash marks on it for every mile per hour, not like the older bus he used to drive that only had marks every five miles per hour.

Yep, fifty-two right on the nose, he'd think.

Sometimes he'd catch up with the engineer in town after an early morning run for coffee. Sadie's restaurant was the place—open early, quiet, decent meals, and no tourists, although there never were any at that time of the day anyway.

"Cold today," the bus driver would say as he drank his coffee.

The engineer wouldn't say much. "Yep. Cold."

"Hey, did you see they changed the rail crossings down there by the old Thompson farm? Real nice signals—can see them a long ways down the highway."

"Yep. Nice."

"I wonder if they scare that dog when they go off," the driver mused.

The engineer stopped for a moment. "Dog?"

"Yeah, that big gray dog I see out there once in a while. Seems skittish as all get-out."

The bus driver looked at the engineer. His face was as white as a sheet. "You okay?"

"Well, I … dog, you say?" the engineer questioned.

"Yeah, in the field out there by the riverbank. You know, where the track goes over that little tunnel."

The engineer was trembling. "That's not a dog."

The bus driver sat silent for a minute. "It's as big as a house. What else could it be?"

The engineer tried to drink his coffee, and the bus driver noticed that the engineer was suddenly terrified.

"It's a rabbit."

The bus driver put down his coffee mug. "A rabbit? Can't be. It's got to be a hundred pounds."

"It's a rabbit. It owns that hole."

With that, the engineer drained his coffee and quickly left.

"Hole? What hole?"

"It owns that hole," the engineer said without looking back as he hustled through the door.

The bus driver read in the local paper a few days later that the engineer had died of a heart attack in the field by his house while splitting wood.

THE LIBRARIAN

T HE LIBRARIAN HAD SPENT all summer cleaning out the old storage rooms and rummaging through the old acid-based paper storage boxes in the basement of the library. He found an entire collection of newspapers from the 1860s and 1870s, still intact. Of interest was a series of articles written about some bizarre occurrences in and around a makeshift sanitarium filled with criminal psychopaths from the Civil War.

One story in particular was intriguing. The article related the reported death of some Confederate soldiers killed by a pack of bounty hunters as they ran to catch a ride on the last train out of the area. They were run down by the hunting dogs and torn apart alongside the train's engine as it rumbled around the bend into the woods. A number of subsequent articles talked about the theory that some bank robbers had held the train's engineer captive while they made their escape from the town and had kept the engineer from slowing enough to let the men catch up and jump on.

Later, other articles were written that relayed more information about three men, each alleged to be one of the bank robbers. Each had died in a different town on the same day. One of them went berserk and ran around screaming about the two red dots staring at him in the night. He ended up setting himself on fire after drinking an entire jug of grain alcohol. The fire on his clothes eventually heated his skin so much it blistered, causing the alcohol in his stomach to explode in a dull thud before engulfing him.

The second man was gored and ripped apart by a feral pig that grabbed his intestines and dragged them all around the area where the man had been hunting for small game in the woods. The third man had fallen into an old deep well that was connected to a nearby pond filled with snapping turtles, and he had been devoured down to the bones in a matter of hours.

The librarian also found an article about a bizarre killing that had occurred on the highway many years later, near the spot where those Civil War soldiers had been hunted down and killed. A man who had been driving with his wife and daughter one afternoon, apparently on their way for a picnic in the woods, suddenly went crazy and killed them both with his bare hands. He then disemboweled himself by ripping through his own skin and hung his intestines out the window of the car as he drove down the highway before he died behind the wheel. When the police finally found the car, some animals had apparently dragged parts of the body out of the car into the open field. The police found a pile of gray fur clutched in his hands.

The librarian took notes and then transposed the locations onto a map of land parcels. He found the spots referred to in the news articles … right by the Thompson place, near the railroad tracks, where the highway passed under.

The librarian felt a chill go up the back of his neck. He knew that place. He knew that spot. He'd seen those red eyes chasing him as a kid.

Without thinking, the librarian picked up the entire bundle of notes and news clippings and hurried down into the basement where he threw everything into the incinerator. He prayed he would never remember that he had discovered anything about that place. He wasn't going to tell anyone about this.

Later that month, he found a new job in another state and moved away. He never even bothered to quit.

THE VETERINARIAN

THE VETERINARIAN HAD LIVED in the same house all of her life. It had belonged to her great-grandmother. The entire family had pretended to be farmers, but they had all been doctors, lawyers, and veterinarians—educated people. And the women in the family had all had a special gift. It was especially strong in the vet herself. Some people just called it a woman's intuition.

She had been born in what would later become her own bed, with her grandmother helping her mother. Her mother had felt like she had been reborn herself and shortly after the birth, much against the advice of the grandmother, had wrapped the little girl in a cotton sheet and walked with her outside. The birth had occurred during a freak storm. The lightning was so bright that it looked like daylight.

The little girl's name was Sara, but there could only be one nickname for her: Sun.

She was from a family of reformed Methodists, a point that the traditional Methodists in the area never forgot, except for the fact that the crops the family raised were much better than anyone else's. The tomatoes were huge and durable, the squash was big and sweet, the spinach was deep green and leafy the way spinach should be, and their corn was the best in the county. They had taken great pride in simple things.

The little girl she had been grew up as a farm girl, learning to milk cows and tend sheep and birth lambs and care for every living thing in the world. She built birdhouses during the winter months, as well as beehives and perches for the family of hawks that had occupied the land for hundreds of years. She raised bunnies for show, but never to eat. Her parents were respectful of each creature's right to make its own way the best way it could and let her do what she wanted to do.

She had a gift for sounds. She could imitate all kinds of birds, even calling in Canadian geese to land and rest near their pond during their long flights south for the winter, away from the hunters. They trusted her.

It was as if the peace of the world had descended on their farm, and it was destiny that she would become a veterinarian. She had worked her way through the local university, which was the only landmark to speak of in that part of the state. The vet did well and tolerated the lessons of anatomy and dissection in order to realize her dream. She spent three more years at veterinary college just across the state line at Lindsay, and when she returned home, she joined the only vet practice for twenty miles in any direction, caring for livestock, farm animals, and pets of every kind.

As she grew into a woman, she realized there was a reason why animals liked her and why they tolerated her probing and prodding and sticking—they sensed she understood them and meant them no harm. She could almost hear them talking to her.

Once she had to care for a horse that had wrenched its leg by stepping into a range hole, nearly breaking it off at the knee. The horse was in desperate pain, and all she could hear was the horse asking if her baby was all right. The vet couldn't understand why the horse would be thinking this.

When the horse's owner came over to the barn, he gruffly spoke under his breath, "Baby's going to be awful sad."

The vet turned quickly to him and asked what he meant.

"Baby. Baby and that horse ain't been apart since Baby was born, rides on her back all the time."

Baby was the cat.

The vet asked where the horse had fallen, and the man pointed out up the hill, over the rise, near a tree. The vet left the horse, now dozing off under a sedative, and walked up the hill to the top of the rise. She stopped and listened. She could hear the sound of a cat crying.

She walked slowly through the area until she heard the cat as loud as if it was in front of her, and she looked down.

There was an old well, maybe fifteen feet deep. The mouth of the well had been boarded up except for one small slot of broken slab. The vet knelt down and pulled the turf away from it.

Baby was there, pacing back and forth, in a near panic.

With the help of a thick rope, the cat practically clawed its way up the rope by itself and then raced off to the barn.

When the vet returned, the cat was sitting next to the horse's face, rubbing itself on him.

The horse survived; the vet would later manage to fix the knee. It would limp a bit and was no good for farm work anymore, but the owner let it live.

Baby was very happy and rubbed on the vet's leg.

"You're welcome," she said.

"Dr. Sun, what's the bill?" the owner had asked.

"On the house. Just fill in that big hole."

"Already done. Thanks."

THE SURVEYOR

T HE SURVEYOR PLACED HIS sighting mechanism and flags on the ground and made a quick assessment of the field. It was big, almost sixty acres across. At the far end of the field, along the riverbank, was his assistant, standing patiently with a long, graduated marker held vertically. The surveyor found the corner monument for the property boundary, leveled the sighting device, and began making calculations.

Off in the distance he heard a train whistle and causally stepped away from the scope to look down along the tracks toward the source of the sound. He couldn't see the train, but he could hear the slowly increasing rumble of the train as it came closer. He recalled the sound of the real steam locomotive from when he was a boy; he remembered it as a kind of whooshing and chugging. The diesels didn't make that kind of sound, and he missed hearing it. Times had changed.

He stepped back to the scope and began sighting on the marker when he heard the sound of the train rounding the curb in the tracks to make its run along the riverbank. Even thought it was probably half a mile away, it sounded like it was nearly on top of him. Through the scope, he spotted the face of his assistant, who had just turned his gaze back from the train to the surveyor, awaiting instructions to move.

The surveyor was about to step away when the noise of the train grew so loud that he instinctively looked up, expecting to see the train right in front of him.

Nothing was there.

He looked back through the scope and noticed that he'd lost the field of view. He thought maybe he'd hit the scope and lost his alignment, but when he checked again, he noticed he was right on target.

"Roy, you joker," he mumbled. "Hey! Get your ass back in the right—"

He stopped as he looked over the top of the scope to see his assistant on the ground, wrestling what looked like a big dog. Arms and legs flailed around for a moment and then abruptly stopped.

The surveyor thought maybe Roy had brought his dog with him and wondered what the fool was doing playing around in the middle of a job.

"Roy! You shit! Get back to work!"

Just then, the surveyor saw the dog turn its head back toward him, and all he could see were two bright red eyes.

The animal was hunched over Roy, holding him down with the sheer weight of its body. The surveyor thought for a moment about running over to shoo the dog away, and as he took a few steps in the direction of the dog, he realized that it wasn't a dog at all.

"What the hell is that? Is that a bear? Can't be—no bears around here anymore." His voice was escalating. "Maybe it's a mountain lion?"

Just then, the gray animal bounded off of Roy's chest, and in its mouth hung the man's intestines, which had been ripped out. With almost no visible effort, the creature dragged Roy's body behind it as it headed for the riverbank.

"Holy shit! Roy? Roy!"

The surveyor began running toward the assistant's body, but partway there he immediately veered over to the truck parked along the highway. He fumbled for a few seconds and emerged from the cab with a shotgun.

He began running back toward the assistant, this time with the shotgun up at his shoulder. As he got to the body, he looked beyond it, down along the riverbank, and saw the gray form sitting on its haunches. The intestines were in its mouth, and it shook its head from side to side, as if it was trying to eat them.

The gray form's eyes snapped onto the surveyor's shape. It lurched forward just a bit, as if readying itself to jump up or lunge at him, but the surveyor leveled the shotgun and fired right at it.

The blast kicked up dust all around where the gray form had been, but it was too quick. It bounded into the brush along the railroad track and vanished.

The surveyor stood, almost in shock, his finger on the second trigger for the barrel with the heavier load in it. He quickly looked around and then backed slowly up to the spot where the body was lying. The entire ribcage had been ripped away, and the face on the corpse looked as if it had been frozen in mid-scream. The hands looked as if they had dug into the fur of an animal; they were still curled at the fingertips.

The surveyor ran back to the truck. Pulling his radio microphone off of its stand, he called for help. As soon as the emergency dispatcher acknowledged the location and circumstances, the surveyor reloaded the empty barrel of the gun, grabbed the leather ammo belt filled with shells, and took a seat up on the top of the truck cab, his legs handing down over the windshield, as he kept his eyes on the riverbank.

He waited. Soon he could hear the sirens coming in the distance, and as he listened, he watched the brush and the riverbank carefully. He knew that scared or wounded animals sometimes went berserk. They were unpredictable and might charge in the least expected direction.

He watched the field as the sound of the sirens came closer, and as he saw the red lights from the police car and ambulance coming down the road, he relaxed just a bit. He set the shotgun down on the roof of the truck, slipped his feet over the side, and slid off.

He turned to open the cab door to grab his wool cap, and as he did so, all he could see in front of him was a burning set of red eyes.

At that exact moment, the breath went out of his body as he heard a ripping sound, like the tearing of old fabric, and felt his chest heave. He found himself looking at his own guts and realized that even though he wanted to breathe, there was nothing left to breathe with.

As the police car pulled up in front of the truck, he fell to the ground. *Bunny Man owns that hole.*

THE PICNICKERS

THE PICNICKERS WANDERED OFF the road and found a path to a cluster of trees through the old wire fence. Their two dogs ran ahead, darting in and out of patches of overgrown shrubbery along the fence line as they searched for rabbits. It was warm, and there was a light breeze floating through the trees, making the early afternoon seem like it existed in suspended time.

The couple spread out a blanket on a flat spot beneath a large tree, situated so they could look out down along the meadow toward the rolling hills on the horizon. They ate and talked and laughed as the dogs wrestled and then rested in the shade of the tree.

"You know, my granddad says that they used to see the ghosts of old dead Confederate soldiers out there at night," the young man said. "His farm used to be right over there along that ridge. Hear them too, at night, calling for help. A few times he'd go out there with the dogs, but he never found anything."

The woman leaned back on one arm and sipped her glass of wine. "Soldiers? Really? I'm surprised."

"Why? There are graves all over this area."

The woman looked out along the meadow. "This was never a battlefield from the war. I learned that at camp." She was teasing him.

"And there's the story about a ghost train rumbling through here, carrying the ghosts of the dead soldiers home. I've never seen it, but people say when you hear train whistles, that it's coming. The regular trains coming through don't blow their whistles around here."

They both drank their wine, smiling at each other over the foolishness of the stories.

Off in the distance the sun started to touch the horizon and seemed to hover there for the longest time before it looked as if layers of it were being stripped away as it sank.

The man and woman watched quietly as the dogs stirred and then trotted back down the path the way they had come.

"It's getting late; we should probably go back." The man stood up and dusted himself off.

The couple gathered up their belongings and started down the trail. Suddenly, the woman realized she'd left her wineglass on the tree stump by the spot where they had been.

"Wineglass," she called out as she turned back up the hill. The man continued on down. Her eyes saw the glass. She reached for it and grasped it by the stem before turning back to the trail.

Her eyes were following the ground before she had even been able to lift a single step when she saw a large pair of feet in front of her. At first she thought it was a dog, then a rabbit, then perhaps a farm animal that had been silently grazing in the meadow. Then she thought it might be a big deer.

But as she began to lift her gaze, the feet seemed to somehow transform into a shape. It was big. It was so close to her she could have reached out and touched it. It was at least the size of a man, but it was almost not a man.

She paused, not feeling afraid, not even startled. For a moment, her mind sent back the thought that perhaps it was the farmer from across the road. Maybe they had been trespassing during their picnic and hadn't realized it.

She couldn't quite see him clearly, as the glare from the sun still shown over the horizon, and it interfered with her sight. But her eyes made their way up from the ground. The figure stood still, and the color of the cloth—or perhaps it was fur—was so muted and faded that it almost looked like the earth around it. But her eyes lifted finally to the face, and she saw two large eyes. They were bright red, almost glowing.

The breath came out of her, as if she had been hit by a punch to the stomach, although she hadn't been. The eyes burned brighter, almost as if they were on fire, and then the eyes faded. What was left was the face of a man—haggard, tired, bearded. His skin seemed old, yet he appeared very fit, like a wound-up spring.

The woman still didn't understand. She didn't feel threatened, just suddenly very cold.

"Are you … are you the farmer from across the road?" The words just seeped out of her.

The face before her was quiet, serene, but at the same time pained. In the next moment, it seemed almost angry.

Behind her, the woman heard the rustling of bushes, but she dared not look away.

She saw the man's face turn just a bit, as if he was looking around for someone to help him, the way a homeless man might when asking for change for a meal he truly needed, well past the point of starvation and hope. He blinked and seemed to breathe. His eyes were far away.

"Can I help you, sir?" she asked.

As the woman spoke, she noticed that he was holding one arm across his stomach, as if he was holding something in. And through the gray fabric covering his body, she saw old blood and a mass of what must have been something he had caught to eat and was carrying under his clothes.

"Are you hurt? Do you need a doctor?"

He breathed hard, almost laboring to take air in and out. In his eyes she saw fear, exhaustion, and pain and a longing for something, like home. He looked like a man stranded in a strange town with no way to get to where he needed to be. He struggled to stand for a moment, and the woman felt he was almost about to speak, when, behind her, one of the dogs barked and scurried back up the trail.

As the dog neared, the man's eyes flared into giant red boils, and as the woman turned to look back down the trail, the shape faded away. She turned back and saw nothing.

In the distance, the sound of a train whistle hovered quietly in the air.

The woman's heart was now racing, and her hand, which had cradled the wineglass for what felt like an eternity, suddenly tightened. The glass stem snapped like a twig, cutting into her hand.

She gasped for air and stepped backward two or three steps, almost out of balance, before she steadied herself.

"Hey, anything wrong?" the voice of the man down the trail called up to her. "You coming?"

The woman suddenly felt faint, and she silently settled to the ground. The man rushed back up the trail to her, the dogs yelping and running alongside him.

"What … what happened?" the man asked.

"I … I … I just …" She tried to get the words out. "I just saw—"

The man looked about as he steadied her. "What?" he asked again.

"I just saw … saw …" The words wouldn't come.

The man lifted the woman and helped her back down the trail toward the meadow, along the path to the fence, and across the road to the car.

"I … I … just saw a …" The woman wretched by the car door and then collapsed into the seat.

The woman felt as if she had been hit by a bolt of lightning and was unable to speak.

THE DOCTOR

T HE DOCTOR'S GRANDFATHER HAD settled in the county when he had returned from the war—the Civil War. His own father had also been a doctor in a town in the next county. The family had been in the area since, well, before the state had been a state. He was proud of that. He had grown up going with his own dad to make house calls, the way country doctors had done—the way he still did.

So when the phone rang on a Sunday evening and it was someone he had known since birth asking for him to come right away, he laid down his fork, kissed his granddaughter on the cheek, and asked his daughter to keep his dinner warm. He took his medical bag and went to the car. He had told the caller to meet him at his office, which was halfway between them.

It was a short drive by country-living standards, maybe four miles up the highway. The doctor arrived first; he turned on the lights and opened up the front door. He had his white coat partway on when the man pulled up. The doctor could see there was a woman in the front seat. She looked sick, but she could walk. The man helped her up the stairs and into the office, where the doctor helped her into a chair.

"Thanks, Doc, for doing this," the man said. "I know it's your only day off."

"Sure, George. This is what I do. So what happened to your lady friend?"

The doctor knew them both. "Lady friend" was the term everybody used to refer to her, and "man friend" for him, as they had been a couple for years but had never quite made it over the hill into matrimony.

The woman looked shaken, almost in shock.

"We were out on a picnic, and just as we were about to leave, something happened to her. I don't know. Food maybe? A spider bite maybe? Not sure. She just kind of fell down and couldn't talk."

The doctor frowned.

"Okay, Ruth, into the examination room," the doctor said as he helped to lift her up. They steadied her as they walked the few steps to the glass door of the doctor's examination room, and the doctor helped her slip up onto the padded table.

"George, would you go put the kettle on? It's around the corner in the kitchen. I think she might need some warm fluids, so let's start with that."

It was a nice way of telling him to leave them alone, so the man slipped out the side door into the corridor.

The doctor flicked on his penlight, held the light up alongside his face, and shined it into her eyes as he held her chin up. The look in her eyes told him a lot.

The joys of being a country doctor were long lost on the rest of the world, but for him, they made all the difference. He knew these people, knew how they lived, and had grown long familiar with the ways of country life. It was an odd thing to see the world in ways not saturated with noise and over-stimulation, but it was just as much being a doctor as anywhere else would have brought him. Patience was his most important tool.

The woman's eyes were wide, almost panicked, but she wasn't trembling.

"Follow the penlight," the doctor directed. "Yes, that's right. Okay, look left. Now right. Did you hit your head on anything?"

"No." The woman finally spoke—the first time in what must have seemed like hours.

"Good, so you understand me. Any ringing in your ears? And can you see equally out of both eyes? Do you feel dizzy or hot anywhere?" He rattled off the questions as he reached around her neck and felt the back of her head, his fingers looking for a tick or perhaps a spider bite.

"No. I'm just a little startled."

"Okay, so can you tell me what happened?"

Being a doctor in a small town meant developing personal intuition much like a bartender and some investigative skill similar to a traffic cop and mixing it all together with the professional training of a healer. The doctor had seen dozens of patients in varying states of fear, embarrassment, guilt, confusion, and even anger and had learned to treat each with due consideration. But this woman, whom he knew well, had been a patient of his over many years. There was something different about her state of mind, like her sense of disbelief had just been broken.

"I ... I saw something."

The doctor paused. "Something? Like something that made you upset?"

The woman nodded.

"Okay. I want you to slip into one of those exam robes over there, and if you don't mind, I'd like to do a complete exam. Could you do that? It won't take very long. I'll call my nurse to come on over to help." His voice was neutral but at the same time reassuring.

"Okay," the woman agreed.

"I'll go see what George is doing in the kitchen. I'll bring back some tea for you?" He was trying to gauge her state of mind.

She nodded again, this time seeming a bit more responsive.

The doctor closed the door behind him as he went through the corridor and over to the kitchen. The man was there, pouring the hot water into three mugs and dunking tea bags into them.

"So, George, where exactly were you this afternoon?"

"We packed a late lunch and went out for a picnic, out there past the old sawmill—you know, that spot of trees off in the meadow. Up the hill from those canals."

"Oh sure—quiet spot. Anything happen out there?" The doctor knew how to ask in a way that left much more room for interpretation than allegation.

"No, we had a nice time, and when it was time to leave, Ruth realized she'd left her wineglass up there on the stump and went back to get it. A few minutes passed, and I went back to check on her, and she was sitting on the ground."

The doctor thought about that. He knew a lot about the people in his care, but he also knew a lot about the places they liked to go. He knew that spot. His father had known people who had had trouble up there as well. There was something about that place.

They talked a bit more, the doctor allowing sufficient time for Ruth to get into her examination gown. When he knocked on the door and reentered the room, he saw her standing in front of a black-and-white photograph of an old locomotive hanging on the wall. She was almost transfixed.

"You like trains, Ruth?" the doctor asked as he began to clean and bandage up her hand.

"Not really. But I know he does."

"He? He who?"

"That man. That man I saw."

With that, the doctor set down the gauze and medical tape and listened.

THE TREASURE HUNTER

T HE TREASURE HUNTER HAD hiked all through the old saw mill area, occasionally finding old balls of shot from the Civil War that had been turned up by the farmer's plow. He'd uncovered all kinds of things with just a little turning of the soil or the pulling up of old wood remnants. He was more careful now than he had been, ever since he had turned over an old tree stump and was confronted by a very large rattlesnake, mad enough to jump right up at him from about eight feet away before recoiling and quickly slithering off.

The morning air was cold, and off in the distance he heard a train whistle. *Odd,* he thought, *there aren't any trains running on these tracks this time of the day. It should be another couple of hours before one comes through. Maybe it's just a reroute rolling upstate.*

The treasure hunter slipped through the gap in the old fence and quickly found himself walking along the canal, looking across into the meadow, when he saw something sticking up out of the ground on the opposite side of the bank. It looked like a root or some kind of tree trunk—he couldn't tell.

He took several steps back and then lunged for the canal, jumping across it without getting even a foot wet. Then he set his waist pack down and knelt by the strange shape jutting out of the soil and grass.

It looked like it could be the hilt of an old sword.

The treasure hunter pulled the grass and the old twigs and leaves away from it and took a closer look. It was a scabbard.

He took his camera from his pack and shot a couple of photographs of the object. When he was done, he began carefully digging around it until he uncovered what looked like a rotted canvas sack with numerous things inside—an old leather belt that had long since dissolved in the soil, the remnants of an old cavalry hat, and some eating utensils, old, twisted, and rusted. And there was one more thing inside what looked like an old buffalo scrotum tobacco sack—a gold watch.

The treasure hunter looked more deeply into the hole he had dug to recover the canvas sack, and there, underneath, was something else. It looked like a bigger hole, going down farther into the soil. He looked inside, but the light was at the wrong angle and he couldn't see without the help of a flashlight. He didn't have one.

He held the gold watch in his hand and rubbed away the tarnish and the mold until he could see that it was a pocket watch with a little cover for a photo inside.

He gently slipped his fingernail under the clasp and popped the watch cover open.

There was a set of photographs of a bearded Confederate soldier with his wife. The eyes of the solider looked distant, and the eyes of the woman seemed to long for his return. The hiker wasn't sure why he felt that, but it suddenly felt very real to him.

Just then, a huge gust of wind blew along the canal bank, stirring up dust, and as the hiker covered his face to protect his eyes, he felt a tug along his waist.

The treasure hunter uncovered his face to be met by a pair of red, burning eyes that seemed to rest on top of an old gray flannel suit.

It looked like a suit. *Or was it an animal?*

The thing had come up upon him so quickly that he didn't have time to be scared. It was so close that he could feel the breath of the thing on his face.

From beneath the red eyes, a piercing scream came forth, and the treasure hunter realized that the thing had hold of him at the waist, and it felt like claws were digging into his skin.

The noise was horrific, but from within the noise was a distinct sound—a word buried within a hissing noise. The treasure hunter heard it clearly.

"Mine."

The treasure hunter struggled to pull away, but the grip on his waist was now almost a death grip, like a giant snake squeezing him.

"Mine!" the voice screeched.

The treasure hunter dropped the watch, and the red eyes receded to reveal the face of a man, his long beard partly gray, his long hair haggard and knotted. As the watch hit the ground, the man let go of the treasure hunter and dropped to his knees, his hands clutching the watch.

"Mine. Mine." The voice transformed into almost a whimper, and then it slowly turned into a sob.

"Mine. Mine!"

The treasure hunter was terrified, but he knelt by the man and spoke to him through his own fear.

"Mister, are you okay? Can I help you?"

With that, the red eyes instantly flared up again and the voice boomed. "Mine. My hole!" The man leapt at him and somehow passed right over him and across the canal, knocking the treasure hunter onto his back.

With that, another gust of wind seemed to blast the canal bank as a freight train rumbled past. The treasure hunter hadn't even heard it approaching until it was practically on top of him.

He found himself sprawled out on the dirt, his waist feeling like it had been crushed by a bear hug. He slowly climbed to his feet, picking up the watch and the canvas sack. In his mind's eye, the image of the photograph remained, and along with it, he heard the man speak again.

"Mine!"

The treasure hunter managed to scramble up along the railway and across the adjoining field to the highway, where he sat for what felt like forever until a feed truck came by. The driver, seeing the man was hurt, stopped and helped him into the back of the truck and drove him up to the town. By the time they arrived, the treasure hunter was feeling a bit better, enough to raise his shirt and look at his stomach. It looked like it had been clawed open by a wild animal.

The driver sat with him for a few minutes until he knew the man was okay.

"You know, that's a nasty scratch. Bear?"

"No, I don't know what that thing was. But it was big—like a man."

"The doc's place is right up over there. There's a phone on the porch you can use to call him; the operator will connect the call for you. He'll come right over."

The treasure hunter nodded and then walked slowly up the street to the doctor's office. He lifted the phone, and the call went through to the doctor. He'd be there in ten minutes.

By the time the doctor arrived, the police were already there.

There on the porch was the gold watch and the canvas bag with all of its contents. The treasure hunter himself had been completely torn apart by what must have been a wild animal.

THE SOLDIER

THE SOLDIER HAD WANDERED for days, weeks, he couldn't be sure. It was cold. The winds were chilling, and the nights were hell, hiding along the banks of the canals that ran all through the area. Sometimes, when he was quiet, he could hear the hounds of the trackers following him. Sometimes they would sound as if they were right on top of him; other times, they were so far away that the barks and yelps of the dogs seemed to almost float on the air, like words spoken in a rainstorm—soft, haunting, almost lyrical, but menacing and ultimately lethal.

He starved most of the time, and the exposure to the elements caused his uniform to go threadbare more quickly than it had during the two years he'd been fighting the war. Now all he wanted to do was to get home, if there was a home. The only thing that helped him to focus was gazing at the photograph of his wife and speaking her name softly to himself. Somewhere, out there, she was waiting, and he prayed she'd still be alive when he finally got back.

He'd traveled in a general southwesterly direction, but after a few days, he was sure he was going the wrong way. He'd see wagonloads of Union soldiers rumble past on their way to reinforce the occupancy of some of the cities that were now under martial law. Once, one of the soldiers on a wagon spotted him and raised his rifle to fire a shot at him, but before he could pull the trigger, one of the others laughed and pushed the rifle up into the air. The fugitive could hear the laughter and some stern words through the sound of the rumbling wagon. "Don't waste it. He'll be dead soon enough."

The weeks wore on … evading, hiding, pretending. He grew gaunt and drawn, his skin now leathery and weathered, his black beard now almost gray, like his hair had become. He looked almost ghostly.

Ghostly. Maybe that's a way to make some headway.

He followed one of the wagons along a trail until it came to the outskirts of a small town. *Seems quiet enough*, he thought. He waited—a day, two days. Watching. The same way he had when he was picking off Union officers in the field. Long after everyone had thought the areas were empty of hostiles, he would fire a shot from so far out that the sound traveled almost to the moon and back. He'd be out of his hide and on the move before he could even see the shot hit. More often than not, it would be answered with vicious volleys from down range, letting him know that he'd been successful.

He'd managed to pick up some scraps of food from a dump on the outskirts of the town—rotten fruit, some rancid meat. But he had to eat. The dogs had picked up his scent for just a moment, but he rolled himself in some road apples and then swathed himself with the carcass of a dead skunk. The dogs yelped later when they came across the spot where he'd smothered himself in foul scent but soon gave up their interest.

He'd long since ditched his rifle and a pistol he'd captured during a battle—too heavy, too loud, too hard to find powder and shot for it, and worthless after it got wet. He knew he'd have a hard time hunting without it, but he couldn't take the chance of firing for game with Union troops nearby. They'd just as soon kill him as take him prisoner. The war was over, but not the fighting.

Or the slaughter.

Finally, he decided he had to break cover and find out where he was. He needed to know how far away the railway was, if the trains were running, and what the latest news of the war was.

He'd spotted an old shack out back along the trees, off the streets of the town, and had seen an old lady sitting in a rocking chair. She was there most of the evening, every evening, whittling or knitting, he couldn't tell which. But he figured his best chance was to just make a move. He couldn't survive much longer.

The evening came when the whole town had looked as if it had congregated on the far side of the municipality, except for the old woman. She was there as usual, smoking her pipe.

He slowly, carefully, lifted himself from his hide and made his way to the edge of the shack. He looked around, even through the window, and then came around the corner of the structure to the porch.

"Heard ya." The woman's voice was almost a cackle.

The soldier bristled, nearly panicked, but he thought he had heard a friendly drawl in the voice.

"No worries. Not gonna tell anybody. You come on out, so I can see ya."

His voice was gruff. He hadn't spoken plainly in a long time, and he struggled to get the words out. "Where am I?"

The lady straightened and then eased herself back into her chair. "You're in blue belly heaven. This here town's called Buckle."

The soldier looked at her face. Her eyes were as white as the sun on a clear winter day.

"I can see you plain. You look like you've had a bit of a trip. There's water there in that pail."

The soldier rushed for it and drank it all down.

"I reckon you're trying to just stay alive, I take no trouble with that. There's ham hanging out back by the little shack; you go slice yourself off some and eat it up. Take some with you. It'll keep."

"Gotta get home," the soldier stuttered.

"There ain't nothing left to get to. Everything's been torched, burned. 'Least around here anyway. Maybe deeper south you'd be okay. But stay off the roads; stick to the woods. And watch out for the skinners."

"Skinners?"

"Yep. Them's rebel soldiers working for the Union hunting down rogues, deserters. Taking men on both sides. You'll hear 'em; I do. They use dogs. They get ten dollars a man or a set of ears, whichever they can bring back. If they catch a rebel soldier, they'll kill him soon as bring him back—too much trouble. And nothing regular paid for the Union men, neither, lest it's an officer. Just good for more blood, I guess; ears all look the same. And it don't matter what kind of blood they get, even women and children being killed for money. Hard to believe, Confederate soldiers hunting down their own."

The soldier felt scared. He felt like an condemned fugitive. He didn't have the strength to keep running.

"Now you never mind those cowards," the woman continued. "You keep on headin' home. There's a train that comes through only once a month, run by a man from Washington. He owns the line, and the Union can't catch it. They say he's a friend of the South. May be the last run this time. Gotta be in the right place at the right time to jump it. It's due in three days. Go west of here another day. You'll see a long road with red soil on it; that's the Blood Trail. Be sure to stay low. Go south a bit, and you'll find a long canal and a spot where the train passes over it on a small bridge with a road passing under it. No other spot like that in these parts. Hide there. The train'll blow its whistle just once as it rounds the bend. After that, it switches tracks and doesn't stop till it's home down South."

The soldier tried to speak but couldn't.

"That's okay. You just get back home to that pretty wife, Sara. She's got a surprise for ya." The woman smiled at him, but the expression seemed almost sinister in its appearance.

The soldier turned and suddenly thought of the ham. He rushed to the little shed and found a whole ham hock hanging inside. He ate through two or three mouthfuls and then took the carving knife from the shelf and cut off a healthy piece. Too much would give the dogs more scent to follow, and they'd be on him again. But he got enough to get to the rail.

With that, he started to make his way to the woods, but midstep he realized he'd never told the old woman about his wife or what her name was. He looked back from the spot where he'd seen the shack plain as day, and it was now dark, empty, broken down. The rocking chair was now a broken pile of wood splinters, and the old woman was gone.

He shuddered but picked up his pace and disappeared into the woods.

THE SKINNERS

THEY PICKED UP THE soldier's scent somewhere back along the garbage dump. It was confusing for the dogs at first, but once they found the spot where the soldier had slept, the dogs had the scent.

One of them charged off toward the old shack at the edge of town and began yelping. As the skinners ran, the dogs perked up.

"Yep, that's one for sure," said one of the skinners. "Never seen Jake run like that. Maybe this'll be the one we've been looking for all this time."

The men ran, some of them with the dogs on long leads; some of them trotting on horseback. They worked their way through the first pass of the woods and then started heading west.

They each wore a holster with a cap-and-ball pistol and carried a sword in a scabbard tossed over their shoulders, along with various bags of gear and bedrolls. Despite the kits, they moved almost silently—and quickly. The dogs sniffed as they ran and kept their barking down.

The men looked up at the sun. "West. Yep, this one's trying to get out," one noted. The men smiled as they ran.

"He won't make it. We got another team out there along the road. I saw a message at the telegraph office back in Baxter that they'd caught more than fifty of these rebs, all waiting for the big train. And they've upped the bounty; it's twenty dollars a head."

"Blue bellies too?" one of them asked as he led the dogs.

"Yep. Blue bellies dead or alive."

They smiled at each other.

"Well, then, let's get going. I got kids to feed."

They picked up the pace, and the dogs charged on ahead.

THE HUNT

THE SOLDIER FELT REPLENISHED from the water and the ham, and he ate what he had left. He'd heard the trackers, the other dog hunters, and had seen too many patrols to take a chance. He figured he could either eat the food now or keep it and get caught from the smell. He ate it as he walked fast.

He moved through a wooded creek and came upon a lone saddled horse that had somehow gotten itself tangled up in some fence wire near the moving water. The horse was mad and had struggled, but it couldn't get loose. The soldier lay quietly for a bit to see if anyone else was around, but no one was. He crept up on the horse, and calming it with his voice, he managed to untwist the wire and let the horse loose.

"Whoa there, Nellie. Bet you want to get out of here," the soldier said. "Me too."

The horse reared back a bit and then steadied itself and immediately walked to the creek and drank for a long time. She limped a bit, but the soldier knew she'd be okay.

Maybe he could ride out of there. He thought long about that but decided against it. *Too loud, too many tracks. Nope, better hike it,* he thought to himself.

Then he thought a bit more. *Maybe … maybe I'll let them think I rode out of here.*

He took his knife and sliced through the straps on the saddle and let it fall to the ground. The horse was unsteady for a moment and then went back to drinking.

He lifted the bridle off the horse's head and pulled it away before tearing a big swatch of wool from his overcoat. He smelled it; it smelled like old socks and skunk. The horse stayed steady as he wetted the swatch from the creek, packed it with moss, and wrapped the wool around the horse's sore leg, tying it tightly enough to cover the wound from the wire.

He hoped the skinners might be distracted long enough to take the wrong scent and go in a different direction. The rag wouldn't stay on for too long, maybe a couple of miles, but that might be all the extra help he needed.

With that, the horse looked at him and then trotted off, avoiding the downed fence wire along the creek and disappearing off to the northwest.

The soldier filled his hat with water, drank as much as he could, and then hurried off through the woods.

Later that day he came to a grove of trees bunched up like a bouquet of flowers. Alongside it was the Blood Trail. It did look red.

He turned south, followed the trail from afar as discreetly as he could until he found the spot the old woman had talked about—the train bridge passing over a very short span, almost like a hole.

He sat in the scrubs, watching, listening. And far off in the distance, he thought he heard a train whistle. He saw shadows moving on occasion way off along the canal; he couldn't tell if they were men or animals, but they never seemed to get any closer.

He was scared. He hoped what the old woman had said was true, and he hoped that she wasn't a collaborator, selling out Confederate soldiers for cash the way so many people had. They'd tried to survive the end of the war, with everything done, everything destroyed, so many people dead.

He didn't move all night, and it felt to be almost bone-chilling cold, but it might have been the fear. He shivered; he tried to sleep. He couldn't. All he could think about was that he was almost out of there, hoping, hoping that his wife was still alive and that he had a farm to return to.

The sun was beginning to warm up the sky. Sunrise was coming. So too was the train—he hoped that was true.

Just then, he heard the barking of dogs and the cantering of horses. He froze, refusing to move. He'd learned that sometimes, if you think the game is really up, you have to force the pursuers to drive you out into the open. Sometimes they knew where you were; sometimes they didn't. He wasn't going to give them a chance to spot him if they hadn't already.

The dogs tumbled past him down the hill and across the canal. The horses were right behind them, with the men on their backs lifting their rifles up to their shoulders as they charged through the water.

The soldier watched as they made for a tall clump of weeds, which suddenly sprung to life and began to run on its own. It was another soldier who had been hiding, waiting for the train. He ran hard, but the dogs caught him in no time. He tumbled to the ground, entangled with the dogs, what seemed like dozens of them.

The dogs snarled and barked and pulled at his flesh, while the men on horseback stopped nearby, watching as the man fought off the animals.

"Do we want this one?" the soldier heard one of the men shout.

"Nah—he ain't worth the effort."

With that, the man lifted his rifle, and calling the dogs off, he shot the man through the head. His body instantly went limp, and the dogs were back on him, tearing away at him. The rider slipped down from his saddle and took a knife to the dead soldier's ears.

"Twenty dollars right there."

The soldier stayed as still as he could, hoping he wouldn't be seen, and waited.

The sun was building off in the distance, and just before the light broke over the rear tree line, he thought he heard the sound of a far-off locomotive. It was a low, churning sound, like a rumbling thunderstorm.

Just then, the train whistle blew—loudly. He realized he'd drifted off. It was almost on top of him; he could feel the rumbling in the ground as the train bore down on him.

He looked up the rail and saw the head of steam and then looked back at the skinners and their dogs. He just needed to wait another few seconds.

The locomotive screamed past him, and he was up and running for the side of the rail cars as they passed by.

All he could think about was his wife, Sara, waiting for him. He struggled to reach the handles of the railing on one of the cars, slipped, and then ran for the next one. Other soldiers who had managed to catch the train were straining to see him as he ran, some of them calling to him, urging him on.

He ran. He ran hard, and as he ran, he sensed the dogs behind him, gaining on him.

"Sara! Sara!" The soldier sobbed as he ran, his hand reaching for the last car as the train began to pick up speed.

And with that last lunge for freedom, the dogs were on him.

The train suddenly disappeared down the track. Some of the soldiers who had escaped shouted back at the skinners, but before the words fell on the open space, the train was gone.

The dogs ripped at the soldier's body, digging into this stomach. The soldier screamed until he was out of air. His lungs were gone.

"How 'bout this one?" the one hunter shouted over the screaming man and the snarling dogs.

"Nope, he's a goner. Just like a rabbit, a spring bunny gettin' eaten! Ha!"

The dogs pulled his innards out, trailing them away from his body and trampling them into the dirt on the bank of the canal.

Somehow the soldier managed to kick the dogs away and pushed himself backward into a small crevice beneath the tracks.

"Look at him, the rabbit's going into his hole!" the man shouted to the others.

The soldier's last thoughts as he died were of his wife, the dogs, and that he was safe in that hole.

He the rabbit. The Bunny Man.

And that his hole.

That his hole forever.

THE LINE

THE SOLDIER HADN'T KNOWN of it, but his wife, Sara, had given birth to a daughter several months after he'd left to fight the Union.

The daughter's name was Sara too, for her grandmother.

The war had gotten too close to the farm, and they had fled farther west to live with the soldier's sister, out of the reach of the Union march and free of the winds of the war that was ripping the country to pieces.

Little Sara grew up fast there, milking cows early in the morning, feeding the hogs, caring for the newborn lambs, and teasing the cats that patrolled the barn and the yards around the house.

Her favorite friend was Blue, a coonhound that trailed her wherever she went.

Of her father, she knew nothing except through the set of photographs her mother kept in a gold frame by her bed. The frame had a glass dome and a gold hook on it where a pocket watch was supposed to hang. And she knew of him by the stories his sister told her; he was a decent man.

The watch was not there. Her mother had asked the soldier to take it with him and to keep it close to his heart.

Sara the mother died of pneumonia when her little Sara was barely six, and with no news of her long-lost father, an honorable man who had served the calling he felt was right, she felt so alone. Her mother's last words were for him.

Back home, the farm they had left out of fear grew into disarray. It became overgrown and was eventually stripped down by the weather to acres of scrub. The house seemed to wilt, to run like a watrercolor painting left out in the rain, the old negro slaves of the plantation staying on to have a roof over their heads.

Someday I'll go back there, little Sara had thought.

Little Sara kept on with her aunt and uncle at her grandparents' house, where she grew up, went to school, and then continued on to college, with her uncle and aunt caring for her as if she had been one of their own. She bore a resemblance to her father … she had his eyes, her aunt said, because of the way they used to seem to be piercing through the night. Her mother had told her it was the gift of seeing in the dark.

And sometimes on windy or stormy nights, she'd hear the sound of a train whistle off in the distance, and she often thought it was the train bringing her father home. She'd often look out beyond the fence and see a gray shape hovering out there. Sometimes she thought it was a deer or Blue or one of the mules wandering around.

She slept in the room that had been her mother's when she had been a little girl, and sometimes at night she thought she could hear the rocking chair on the upper veranda creak back and forth, the way it had when she was a baby and her mother had rocked her to sleep or to help her feel better when she was sick.

She was never scared, only hopeful that her mother was there, watching over the farm and waiting for her missing husband to return.

Sara herself eventually married, and with the help of her new husband, a lawyer and newly elected state judge, she laid claim to the old farm the family had left behind during the war and began renovating it. It had long since been abandoned, the roof caving in upstairs, but they worked hard at it. After several months of rebuilding, lot clearing, plowing, and seeding, they went out to the fence on a Sunday evening and surveyed the farm. The old homestead had emerged from the brush and thickets to stand as it had once been. It was her home, the place that Sara hoped her parents might be able to see from heaven.

And it was here that the next young Sara was born.

This Sara lived the same life, milking the cows, collecting eggs from the roost, and learning to love the animals of the farm. She was a natural student and loved to read. She explored, too. Her favorite dog was Tick, one of old Blue's descendants, who followed her everywhere.

And as Sara grew up, did her schoolwork, and lived the life of a smart, shy country girl, she realized that animals loved her the way she loved them.

So when it became time to go to college, she picked her courses and set her plans in motion. It was off to veterinary school.

Her own daughter, Sara Jane, was born during a long, cold winter in the middle of a freak storm that no one who lived there had ever experienced before, but memories of a storm like it long in the past lurked in the hushed words of the oldest neighbors. It was a warm lightning storm in the middle of the cold night, with thunder so loud and lightning strikes so bright they lit up the entire farm. And for the first two hours of Sara Jane's new life, the temperature rose just enough to allow her dad to birth some lambs in the barn. Her mom would have been there to help too, except she was busy bringing little Sara Jane into the world.

Those lambs and Sara Jane were later inseparable and became known as the kids.

And because of the bright light that shown outside at her birth, light that her mother clearly remembered making the bedroom brighter the moment her daughter was born, Sara Jane had a nickname: Sun.

THE CORONER

THE COUNTY CORONER HAD all the body parts that had been collected from the doctor's porch spread out on the metal autopsy table. Somehow, in the artificial light of the room, they looked almost fake—a foot with a shoe on it, ripped off the bone just above the ankle; an arm, twisted into an unnatural shape, as if it had been bent like an old coat hanger; a ribcage, ripped open; and, of course, the head, which stared up into the lights, its expression one of sheer terror.

"Never seen this before," the coroner said to the sheriff. "I've seen lots of farm accidents, men who fell into thrashers or hail bailers, all twisted up and trussed up like chickens getting spit out of the back end, but never anything like this."

"So, what do you think?" The sheriff was pensive. He knew what *he* thought. "Wild animal?"

"Never seen anyone killed by a wild animal that wasn't drug off and eaten."

"Dogs?" The sheriff's voice went up hopefully.

"Dogs … well, they do stuff like this, but look at the victim. This was a man who was in good shape, fit. Hell, all he'd have to do was land one good kick to the head of a big dog, and he'd probably knock it out. And there's no blood out there. Animals that kill for fun love the blood. No blood out there."

"Well, shit, Irv, then what the hell happened to this guy? He just got ripped apart by somebody passing a beer fart from across the street? Come on, help me out here."

They both looked at the parts spread out on the table but didn't speak. Then the sheriff rose, placed his notepad on the chair, and went over to the other table. There on the table were the hiker's belongings—his pack, some coinage, and the canvas sack.

"What's this?" the sheriff asked.

"Well, that was there with him on the porch. Looks like he was carrying it."

The sheriff looked over the canvas sack, this time more closely. "Looks too old. You look inside of it?"

"Nope, not my department," the coroner said as he lifted the foot with the shoe on it, noticing the red soil in the tread of the sole. "Hey, there's red soil here."

"So, he'd been out along the Blood Trail."

"Yep."

The sheriff nodded and then returned his attention to the canvas sack. He pulled the mouth open and carefully dumped out the contents.

The buffalo scrotum pouch with the gold watch made a clink as it slid onto the table.

The sheriff carefully opened the pouch and placed the watch in his hand. "Man, look at that. Haven't seen anything like that except in a museum."

He popped open the cover on the watch, looked at the timepiece itself, and then turned it over to look at the back side. He slid his fingernail under the cover of the back and slowly popped it open.

The photographs of the soldier and his wife were there, like they had been frozen in time.

"Well, I'll be … look at this, Irv."

Just then, the lights in the room went black.

"Power short," the coroner noted. "Damn, that old circuit breaker. City was supposed to get that fixed for me."

"I'll get it," the sheriff said as he placed the watch on the table and walked through the swinging door down to the rear of the building.

"It's right there by the back door. You'll see the switch cover," he heard the doctor say loudly from back up the hall.

The sheriff found the panel and was about to throw the switch when he saw something, or someone, hovering out back. The sheriff slowly turned toward the window in the door and carefully looked out back.

He could see a figure, a man, standing up, leaning against a fence post. The man's head hung low, his hands covering his face, as if he was sobbing. He had a long beard and long hair, all almost gray, but beneath it he seemed to be a young man. His hands were rail thin, with long fingers. His clothes were worn-out, almost falling off of him, and he looked as if he was in great pain, the way hoboes looked when they hadn't eaten, slept, or been free of fear for a long time.

The sheriff held his breath for a moment and then pushed through the door out onto the rear porch of the building. As the door swung open, the man looked up for just a moment. And then, all of a sudden, he seemed to just fade away.

The sheriff looked around, startled, but his hand never went near the butt of his gun. He looked again and then went back inside, found the circuit breaker panel, and ran his hands down the row of switches until he found the right one, flipping it back on. The lights in the autopsy room came on, and he could see them shining through the windows up above the hallway.

The sheriff went back up the hall to the autopsy room, swung through the door, and headed back to the table where the hiker's belongings were. He held the watch in his hand, looking at the photographs. Suddenly, he put the watch down and quickly ran through the door to the rear porch again, punching through the doorway until he was outside.

The sheriff stopped, swinging his head in both directions.

"Mister! We've got your stuff in here. You want to come get it? It's okay, no one's going to hurt you." The sheriff held his breath.

Nothing.

"Hey! Mister!"

Nothing.

With that, the sheriff slipped back inside and returned to the room.

"Who you yelling at, Cal? Ain't nobody out there."

The sheriff held the watch in his hand and looked at the photographs again. "Yep, that's him," he confirmed aloud.

"Him who?" the coroner asked.

"That's our man."

THE JEWELER

The Jeweler cradled the watch in one hand as he slipped a blunt blade under the rear cover.

"See there? There are two covers on these. That's a Kestrel, made in Germany. Very few of them made. This watch is probably nearly two hundred years old. Be able to tell you for sure in a minute. Never seen one in this kind of shape, though. It's probably worth a lot of money. Looks almost brand new."

The sheriff watched as the jeweler worked carefully to free the inside plate cover. A small pop was heard as the cover came free.

The jeweler studied the watch thorough the magnifier loop attached to his glasses. "Yes, sir, there it is: 1747."

"How'd you know that?" the sheriff asked.

"Every engraver and watchmaker back then always carved little notes in the rear cover of each watch they handled, dates when it was repaired, you know. It's a code for the trade. You'd never see them without a loop. They just look like little scratches. See here—" The jeweler lifted a larger magnifying glass up to the watch, and the sheriff looked through it.

"See that right there? That's the first engraver's notes on the watch. This one's been in Savannah."

"Germans in Savannah?"

"Lots of them before the American Revolution. Some of them were mercenaries left over from the war who stayed on. Or maybe someone carried the watch here as a present. Lots of immigrants went to the South. This was somebody's wedding gift, probably a mom to her daughter. Let me look a bit more."

As the jeweler went back to looking more closely, the sheriff looked about the shop.

"So where'd you get this, Sheriff?" the jeweler asked as he worked.

"It's from that boy who was killed over there on the doc's porch."

"Reckon it's his?" the jeweler asked.

"Don't know. Got to think about that."

"Loot from a robbery, maybe?"

"Don't know." The sheriff's face was stern. "No robberies I can think of that netted this kind of thing."

The jeweler made a note of all the engravings and then lifted his head up and pulled the loop away from his eyes. "Sara," he said.

"What? Sara who? I mean, what?" the sheriff asked.

"Name of the woman who bought it, maybe. Might even be the name of the girl in the picture too. You know, the one in the photograph. It's damned hard to get those photographs in there, you have to take the thing apart to do it, so likely a jeweler did for them. The name Sara is carved in here twice."

"Okay, that's a start."

With that, the sheriff took the watch, slipped it into an evidence bag, and left.

THE PHOTOGRAPHER

THE SHERIFF HAD THE picture of the locomotive from the doctor's office under his arm as he went into the photographer's studio. He'd had a hunch about things, and he wanted to do some checking.

The photographer's studio had been there since before the turn of the century. Business wasn't so good because it was an expensive service to buy, but the man who ran the shop was also a photo restorer. He knew as much about the local history as anybody else; he'd seen it all through the old pictures people brought in to be repaired.

"So what you got there, Cal? A family heirloom?" he asked.

The sheriff swung the photograph up onto the counter and set it gently down.

"What do you know about this?" the sheriff asked.

"That's the Waxman—only known photograph of it in operation. Lots of locomotive portraits out there. It was a popular thing to do for these wealthy railroad barons back then, but most of those where shot by the manufacturer on delivery day. That shot is the Waxman actually making a run. That's from the doc's office."

"How'd you know that?"

"Well, hell, Cal, look at the back cover of the frame. That picture was framed up and prepared by this shop. See the embossed stamp? Course, I was a boy back then, but I remember going across the street with my granddad and measuring the wall to mount it."

"Anything special about it?" the sheriff asked.

The photographer sat still for a moment, thinking about it. "About the photograph itself or about the train?"

"Well, how about each one."

"That engine was built in Germany—very expensive. Brought here I think in the 1830s by the Waxmans of Albany, New York. It serviced their line down to south of Savannah until just after the war. They had their own rail, private-like. That particular engine ran at a much lower temperature, something to do with the kind of steel used in forging it—made it quieter."

"And the train?"

The photographer instantly grew a bit unsettled. "Lots of stories about that train. The Waxman was the train that ran along the Blood Trail. The stories were a bit ghostly, especially after that last run of soldiers back down South."

"What run?" The sheriff was suddenly feeling unsettled.

"The Waxmans were powerful people. They had hundreds of families depending on them for jobs and keep and such down there, and Old Man Waxman figured he'd be out of business down South if his entire labor pool was murdered trying to get home to their farms. So he had some runs made. Took slaves up North and brought Confederate soldiers back South, ahead of the skinners and the bounty hunters. The politicians in Washington put up with it because he was saving freed slaves, and they turned a blind eye on the rebel running."

"So you said the stories were odd. What did you mean?" the sheriff prodded.

The photographer hesitated.

"Murph, come on, I'm trying to solve a mystery here." The sheriff grinned as he nodded to the photograph. "Tell me what you know."

"Well," the photographer started out, "there was a final run after the war. My granddad told me this. Some Confederate soldiers got picked up right there out by the canal, you know that spot—the clump of trees on the other side of the field, that weird train bridge, you know that spot, right?" The photographer pointed to a large landscape photograph of the spot that hung on the wall across the room.

The sheriff did indeed know that spot, although he had been hoping the story wouldn't go that direction. He nodded.

"The story was that some men got left behind, or got caught by the bounty hunters right at the last minute, and the train left without them. Didn't stop, couldn't stop, whatever. And that some of the men, well—" The photographer swallowed. "Some of the men … got … tortured and slaughtered. Horrible stuff. The train blew its whistle as it rolled out of sight down the switch to the private track and never came back for them."

The sheriff was silent as he thought.

"The story now is anytime you hear a train whistle, something bad is gonna happen." The photographer paused. "This something important? I mean, it happened a long time ago."

"Left behind," the sheriff said under his breath. "Anything else?"

The photographer hesitated and then spoke slowly. "I've never seen it, but I know some folks who have. There's a big gray dog that lives out there. You know Vern Thompson and that piece of farmland he's got way out in the middle of that stretch of road, away from the main farm? Lots of people have seen that dog. Men on the rail trip seem to come across it in the morning. Nobody's ever been able to find that dog except from either driving along the road or riding that rail line. I've been out there myself with Vern hunting pheasants, and we've never even seen any scats. It's like it doesn't exist."

"That isn't a dog."

The photographer could see that the sheriff looked startled, but his voice was calm.

"What do you mean?" the photograph questioned. "You've seen that thing yourself?"

"That isn't a dog." The sheriff's voice grew cold, and with that, he took the photograph from the counter and left the shop.

THE PALM READER

THE SHERIFF SAT IN his truck down the street from the palm reader's shop. He'd driven his own vehicle because he didn't want to be seen entering the shop looking like he was on official business, even though he was. He'd even worn street clothes, no uniform. He waited until around two o'clock, when he knew that everyone else on the street would either be distracted with other things or taking an afternoon nap. Two o'clock was an in-between time when sleep, or distraction, allowed the world to pass unnoticed.

He looked all around him before he opened the door and stepped out onto the street.

The palm reader had been there since the 1890s. A caravan of gypsies had wandered its way all up and down the eastern seaboard, having fled Europe for happier and potentially more fruitful America. Some of them had stopped here, made camp, been allowed to stay, and eventually blended into the town.

The shop was run by three generations of women. There were no men left in the family, as they had all been driven off by the law or else been killed in vendettas with other gypsies. Some of them had simply disappeared. How they kept their family alive was a mystery.

The sheriff grasped the doorknob and pushed through into the outer room. The air there had a scent of incense and dust and felt thick, as if it was filled with memories—or information.

No one was there.

He waited a few moments and felt compelled to leave, having a brief thought that what he was doing was silly and thinking that if a suspect was ever brought to trial, he would be ridiculed into retirement. But something told him he needed an edge, some kind of advantage to use to find out what was really going on in his county.

There was a velvet cord hanging by the threshold into an inner room.

On it was a small plaque that read: Ring. The sheriff stepped forward and pulled lightly. He heard a chime in an even deeper inner room and then the soft sound of footfalls.

A young woman, thin, with dark hair and a beautiful, almost haunting, face came out. She was modestly dressed and had her long hair bound lightly down around her back. Her eyes, the sheriff noticed, were almost luminescent.

"Sheriff, how are you?" The young woman's voice was steady and deep but at the same time almost musical and somehow calming.

"I … I, uh, need some help with something." His tone was flat, not businesslike but also not passive. It was clear he had something to discuss. "But maybe I need to talk with your mother."

"Ah. Fate. But perhaps we were meant to talk—you ever know." She smiled.

They stood silently, facing each other.

The woman paused before she spoke again, not really seeming to be sizing him up. "Of course. Please, come in."

She motioned into the inner room, to a chair along the wall. She took a seat in a small chair by a table in the middle of the room. "Yes."

The sheriff was silent for a moment and then looked about the room. "Yes? I mean, yes. Yes to what?"

"I was just answering one of the spirits here, asking me if you were sincere in your heart about the information you were looking for. He said that this is very dangerous for you. I said yes."

"Spirits. Here? Well, I—"

The palm reader spoke slowly. "Your great-aunt was nicknamed Tillie. She had a small dog named Tillie as well, a Yorkshire terrier. They lived in a three-story farmhouse painted white with gold leaf trim, and from the outside, there was this roof eave that always attracted a wasps' nest."

The sheriff was unsettled for a moment. "Yes, that's right."

"She was a big, strong woman. Your aunt says that she once had to rescue you from the well. You had fallen in, and the rope wouldn't hold you to climb out."

"That's true. I guess I came to the right place."

The woman turned her head slightly to the left, as if she was listening to something. "Your aunt also says that you know what's really going on here."

The sheriff thought about that for a moment. He did know what was going on, but he was reluctant to admit it. He shrugged his shoulders slightly and looked away.

"You have a book, a scrapbook, with newspaper articles and letters in the desk of your office. You have all the understanding you need except for the one piece of information that would have it all make sense. Or perhaps you need some extra help?"

The sheriff nodded.

"So what is your question?" The woman's voice seemed far away.

"I think that the spate of killings we've had here have all been perpetrated by the same person."

The woman listened without responding.

"And I think that the killings are all related to something having to do with the last run of the Waxman, along the Blood Trail. There was a man left behind who may have been tortured by some bounty hunters, and I think that it's his spirit that is doing this. He lives out by—"

"The canal, along that small trestle bridge and that little road passageway," the palm reader interrupted.

The sheriff paused.

"The hole." Her voice was calm.

"And I … the hole?"

"That's his hole." The woman's eyes were ablaze.

The sheriff was silent.

The hole. The train.

"And there's light there too. Sun. It comes from a long line of spirits trying to bring him home." The woman's voice sounded almost lyrical, melodious.

Just then, the sound of a whistle grew, and the sheriff heard it clearly. He tensed. It was subtle at first, but it built until he recognized it as the sound of a tea kettle on the stove. Once he recognized the sound, he relaxed.

"See? You knew the answer." The woman smiled. "Let me go get that. I'll be right back."

The woman rose almost effortlessly and went through a passageway into the rest of the house. As she moved past him, the sheriff realized that as she went by, he couldn't really get a good look at her. She was incredibly beautiful, but at the same time, she was difficult to see all at one time. The details of her appearance seemed to slip away from him.

The sheriff heard the whistle abruptly stop and then heard the noise of a cabinet door opening and closing. The sheriff occupied a few moments looking around the room. There was memorabilia from all around the world—trinkets, really. Some photographs.

He was looking away as the sound of a tea tray, with its china cups lightly rattling, came into the room.

"You know," the sheriff began, "I really didn't think—" He stopped cold.

An elderly woman, much different, was before him.

"Sheriff, so nice of you to come. How can I help you?" The woman's eyes were dark, almost empty.

"I was just telling your granddaughter that—"

The woman's face changed ever so slightly. "I'm afraid you have me at a loss. There's no one else here."

The sheriff looked beyond her, through the next room into the passageway. "But I was just talking to a young woman." He suddenly felt a cold grip on his shoulders. For a moment, he was tightened up with something like fear, but it passed quickly.

The sheriff looked around the room, and his eye was caught by a photograph of the young woman in a silver picture frame among a number of other photographs. He rose up and pointed to the photograph. "There she is."

The woman smiled. "That's my great-grandmother, Alva Alicia. She died many years ago in childbirth." The woman's eyes were hopeful, brighter than before.

"I don't understand. I—" the sheriff suddenly felt ice cold.

The woman smiled but was silent for a moment. Then she spoke in a low, almost unearthly voice. "Fate. Everyone gets the message they need to hear when they come here."

The sheriff immediately felt the need to get outside, away from the room. He dipped into his coat pocket and took out a folded twenty-dollar bill and left it on the table.

"You should come back. We can talk more about that. Tillie has many things to tell you, especially about the corner of the barn that caught fire. There's something out there for you."

The sheriff nodded to her as he turned the doorknob. He went through the door and headed out onto the sidewalk. The last few steps out of the house were labored, almost as if his feet grew heavier and heavier as he tried to walk. The final step out the door was nearly impossible to make. With one desperate push, he forced himself through the door to the outside.

As soon as the sun hit his face, he felt relieved. As he walked back to his truck, he was struck by the urge to look back at the house. As he did so, he saw the elder woman wave to him from a ground floor side window.

But something caught his eye on the second floor, and as he looked up, he felt a cold chill again grip him. He saw the young woman pulling aside the lace window cover, her eyes locked onto his. She held his gaze there for a moment and then nodded her head and smiled. He saw her mouth the name Sara.

He nodded back and lifted his hand in a wave.

There is something powerful at work here, he thought. He needed to keep his wits about him. He straightened, and the cold shiver in him disappeared.

He looked away, and when he glanced back at the upper window, he saw nothing. The window shade was still; not even a breeze coming through the open window disturbed it.

The sheriff got into his truck, started it, and slowly made his way out of town.

THE BARN

T HE SHERIFF DUG ALONG the base of the outer wall of the barn. The kerosene lamp glowed lightly. It wasn't quite completely dark yet, but the shadows cast by the lamp were quickly emerging with the world of night. The birds were singing so loudly that the air seemed to vibrate.

It had been a long while since he'd been out to the old homestead. His brother and his brother's wife were away visiting friends in another county, so he was undisturbed.

He guided the shovel carefully as he went, and after several minutes, he heard a clink as he slipped the shovel into the dirt. The sheriff carefully dug around the object with a long knife, patiently removing layers of hard dirt and rock until he could remove the object.

It was a glass soda pop bottle. It was still capped. He scraped away the dirt and the muck until he could read the label. It read: Whiz-Bang. He remembered the name. It had been a long time since he'd thought about it.

He was about to toss it aside when he heard another sound, a kind of rattling noise from within the bottle. He held the bottle up to the light and saw a momentary flash of gold. He gripped the cap of the bottle in his hands and gently pried it off, setting the cap aside, and then he turned the bottle upside down.

A gold train whistle dropped into his hand. As it touched his skin, he felt a jarring, almost like an electric shock, that jolted him upright.

Things suddenly, almost instantly, grew very quiet around him. The insects had stopped buzzing; the evening birds had stopped singing. And there, along the edge of the barn, down near the back, the sheriff could see a shadow. It hovered there for a moment and then faded into the night.

THE JUMP

THE SHERIFF'S INVESTIGATION FINALLY took him to the moment where he knew he had to go out and see the canal. He went over the information he had while he rode on horseback through the scrubs. He had the sense that something very important was going on, maybe even something he wouldn't be able to explain, but whatever it was, it had to be solved. He needed to see that place along the railroad and get a sense of ... well, something. He didn't know what.

He made his way across the canal, up the dirt road, and through the back end of the clump of trees. He saw a few makeshift campsites and lots of fire pits, but as he made his way down the trail, the scene seemed to change. It looked more and more barren, devoid of human presence, almost lost, like a faded painting, unfinished. He experienced the same sensation far out in the back county, well off the highways and farming roads, where the earth simply looked like a place without people. The sensation chilled him just a bit. It looked like a place people weren't ever meant to be.

As he rode along, he continued to feel the need to look behind him as he passed through bush or crossed a rise in the land. He couldn't help but think there was something just not right. He tightened his elbow against his body and felt the bulk of his pistol riding in its holster.

He looked at his watch. It was almost seven o'clock in the morning.

Far off in the distance, way down across the field toward the canal ahead of him, he saw the funny little hole in the stone wall where the road passed under the railroad. From where he was, it looked like a black spot, like a hole in an old photograph. He didn't pay it any attention.

He loped along, looking for tracks, footprints, anything along the way. There'd been a strong storm that week, and no one had been out there as far as he could tell.

Nothing seemed to be out of the ordinary. He saw some dove feathers in a bunch along the trail, probably caught by a fox. He saw some mouse tracks, little hops in the dust, so small they looked almost like elf steps.

Elf steps. He remembered his grandmother telling him that story. At night, the elves would come out and water the flowers and care for the animals of the woods, and all they'd leave behind was good will and elf steps.

He smiled. Remembering that made him feel good.

Far, far off in the distance, he saw the steam plume of a train headed his way. It was so far off he couldn't tell which line it would wind up on; there were a few switches in between. But the plume was getting bigger. He couldn't hear it yet, but he would shortly.

He realized he had forgotten to look at the rail schedule, which lay undisturbed on his dining room table.

The horse sauntered down the trail into the field, and the sheriff found himself in a spot that was partially scrubbed over. He looked about and then noticed a spot on the ground. It looked like a nest, a place where an animal, maybe livestock, had bedded down for the night. But there weren't any hoof marks there, not even a tail drag.

That's odd, he thought to himself.

Just then, the sheriff heard the train whistle blow far off in the distance. The sound quietly began to float along in the air, lifting, descending, wavering.

He didn't see the shape move toward him at first. It blended in almost perfectly with the field, but the horse saw it, and his ears turned forward quickly. The sheriff noticed as the horse tensed.

The horse stopped and then suddenly shifted its weight back on its rear legs, as if to jump. The sheriff steadied the horse and picked up the movement coming toward him at the last possible moment.

Something hit him. The impact was so hard that he slid right off the saddle and hit the ground all in one motion. The horse shrieked, reared back, and ran off, stopping a few dozen yards away to look back before galloping down the field to the canal and jumping across to the fence where it suddenly stopped dead in its tracks.

The sheriff was stunned, and he fought to right himself as he lay sprawled in the dirt. But as he looked up, he saw a pair of burning red eyes so close that he couldn't see around them.

"Mister! I've got your—" The sheriff gasped and tried to catch his breath.

The sheriff saw a face behind the eyes, just for a moment, and he almost thought that he recognized it. But then he was struck again and hit the dirt hard on his back. Before he could say any more, a set of claws raked across his throat, almost tearing his head right off.

"Mine!" The voice was almost piercing.

That was the last thing the sheriff heard before he died.

That Bunny Man's place.

THE FIND

T HE PHONE RANG IN the vet's office.

"Dr. Sun, it's the sheriff's office," the front desk help called through the doorway.

"The sheriff?" the vet asked.

"No, not the sheriff. It's his office."

The vet set down the chart she had been reading and picked up the phone. She said hello and then listened.

Her face slipped away from its usual rosy self to an ashen, almost morbid complexion and then back again.

"Okay, where is this? Down by the canal … which one? Oh, right, by that stretch of Vern Thompson's. Yes, I know it. I'll come right away."

She hung up and then hesitated for a moment before reaching for her bag.

"Got to go," she announced. "There's been an accident; the sheriff's been killed. Fell off his horse." She withheld the true details, not quite believing them herself.

She was met with a blank stare from her office help. "The sheriff … what? Killed?"

The vet struggled to maintain control. "I'll be back as soon as I can. Call Dr. Kendall over in Wilsey and ask him to come over for a bit to cover for me. If he's busy, check with Dr. Jann's office. Tell Shirley I'll owe her a favor."

With that, she took her jacket off the coat stand and went quickly out the door.

The drive to the canal gave her some time to think. Mostly she thought of the sheriff ripped apart. Her friend of many years was dead. But she also thought about his horse, Nellie, which she had delivered in a barn fifteen years earlier. According to the deputy on the phone, Nellie had been mauled and was in a bad way.

When she got there, there were several vehicles—some state police, the local news photographer, and a couple of local farmers. Vern Thompson was there, standing quietly up on the road. This was Vern's land, she remembered. Most of the men were up near where the sheriff had been killed, but a few were down by the canal. She could see the horse's head standing high, like she was resisting something. The vet hurried down to the horse.

As she got closer, she could hear the horse literally screeching. The men were restraining her as best they could, but the horse was straining.

The vet yelled ahead, and one of the men waved back to her. The men immediately backed away from the horse.

As she got closer, she could see that one of the horse's ankles had been gnawed almost down to the bone. The tendons in back where exposed, and the tissue was nearly shredded. And she could hear the horse screaming for help.

"Okay! Okay. Let's just—okay! Nellie, it's okay." The vet slipped up under the horse's neck and felt her pulse. It was racing.

The vet checked the horse's eyes and saw that they were dilated as wide as they could possibly be. She gently caressed the horse's neck and calmed her down as she looked the horse over. Besides the ankle, there was a deep scratch across her back, almost like a slash. It was clean at the top, as if created by something sharp, and then it seemed to change down lower toward the rump, to something blunter. The vet touched the flesh with her fingers, and the horse reared up.

"Whoa! Whoa. Okay, just relax."

The vet sprayed some aerosol analgesic on the wound and then again around the ankle, and the horse calmed down. The vet added some skin lube to the deep scratch, and as one of the men steadied the horse, she wrapped the ankle in a tight surgical dressing before giving Nellie a shot of tranquilizer from her bag.

She was about to turn away when she heard Nellie say, "Rabbit hole."

The vet spoke back to her in her own mind. "Rabbit hole." The horse's ears came forward, intent on the words. The horse almost seized up again, frantic to escape, but the vet kept her under control.

The vet had towed her horse trailer down behind the truck, and with the help of the others there at the scene, she gently led Nellie back up the way and into the trailer. When the gate was finally closed, the horse seemed relieved.

The vet watched her for a few minutes and then went back to the canal. She looked around for a long time while the investigators photographed and collected evidence. She was looking for rabbit holes.

The photographer, who doubled as the local press photographer, finally came down to see her after he was done.

"Murph, did you see any rabbit holes between here and there?" The vet looked back up the field toward the clump of trees.

"No, I was too busy—" the photographer started.

"No rabbits out here." They both heard the words from behind them. It was Vern Thompson. "No rabbits out here—haven't been since as long as I can remember. Been hunted out, I suppose. No grouse or marmots, either. Used to be, but they're all gone now."

The vet noticed the look on Vern Thompson's face. He looked almost transparent, like a projection. His eyes were nearly as white as the sun.

The vet pulled her eyes away from him and slowly looked around. There was something nearly unnatural about all of this, and she struggled to maintain some lucid attention.

No rabbits? That was unusual. It was an open field, lots of water, scrubs, no trees nearby for hawks to roost. It should have been a good place for rabbits.

"I wonder why." She looked at the farmer as she spoke.

He didn't answer. He just shook his head.

With that, she went back to her truck and drove back to the office, gingerly unloading Nellie into the care shed in the rear. She spent several hours stitching up her flesh wounds and trying to salvage the ankle. With the help of the other veterinarian, they managed to keep it attached.

"So what do you think?" the other vet asked her as they cleaned up.

"Well, looks like it could have been a snare on the ankle, maybe an old wound that got caught up in some fencing wire. The back, though—that's a different deal. Maybe she got cut passing through a fence or a thicket. It almost looks like she was hit with a meat hook or a big tractor claw. But I can't figure out why Nellie didn't just kick if she was being attacked. Horses don't just stand around and let things eat them."

"Unless they're really scared, of course, then they don't want to move." The other vet was pensive.

"Scared? Hell, she's a horse. They run from everything; that's their reflex. They're like birds. Distance doesn't mean anything. Miles are nothing. Why did she stay?"

"I don't know. But maybe there's something out there she wanted you to see."

With that, they cleaned up the surgical bay, and the other vet left.

Sun washed up, checked on Nellie one more time, and then called it a night. But before she went to her weekday sleepover bedroom off of the rear of the office where she stayed when she had animals to look after, she asked Nellie again. "Rabbit hole?"

Nellie's eyes widened for just a moment, and then the words came back. "Red eyes."

THE PASTURE

THE IDEA THAT THE horse was trying to say something with its unwillingness to flee from the attack stuck with Sun. Maybe there was something to that.

An attack? An attack by what? What for?

Several weeks seemed to pass very quickly, without incident. There were no strange killings, no freak accidents, no ghost sightings, and no bizarre storms. And there were no leads in the strange death of the sheriff, the treasure hunter, or any of the other cases. For a few weeks, state investigators scrambled all over town, but eventually the investigations slowly tapered off.

Nellie's ankle healed well, well enough that Sun let her out into the back pasture off of the field by the office to get some fresh air. Nellie galloped off, not even favoring the torn ankle, and quickly found herself among other horses grazing in the pasture.

Sun sat on the rear porch, drinking a glass of lemonade and watching the horses run and wander, when her eyes caught something off to the side of the hill.

At first, she couldn't tell what it was. A deer, maybe. It slowly crept closer to the small herd of horses, but it would stop and stand so still that it faded into the background.

Sun watched more closely, almost straining to see. Then, without notice, Nellie galloped off toward the shadow, or the thing, whatever it was. Nellie stopped abruptly in front of it, her head held high and back, as if she recognized something, but she could tell that Nellie was startled.

Sun stood, leaning over the railing of the porch, straining to see. Nellie was frightened, she could tell. She looked more closely.

Something was holding the horse in place.

Sun leaped off the porch and began moving quickly into the field, running toward the horse. As she got closer, she could see a set of legs behind Nellie, standing in place, as if someone were standing beside her but on the opposite side, with the horse's body obscuring whatever it was.

As Sun got even closer, she could see a set of gray-trousered legs and some leather boots, worn, split, and torn. Nellie's head was lower now; she was less scared than before. She seemed to be listening to something.

Sun closed to within about fifty feet, when Nellie suddenly bolted and ran off the other direction.

Sun stopped and saw a shape standing there—a man … a gray man. His expression looked tired, sad, lonely. His old gray field coat was moldy, ripped, torn, and threadbare. His hair and beard were long, not like someone who had grown them out for fashion, but like someone who had been deprived of the chance to keep himself groomed.

The man watched the horse run off, and then, lowering his head, he paused just a moment, as if he was contemplating his fate. It was almost as if he had failed to see Sun standing there. Suddenly, his head snapped up, and he looked at her, his eyes fierce and angry.

Sun was startled, but she held her breath. Without saying a spoken word to him, she asked him with her inner voice if he was tired, the way she often asked animals who were wounded or in labor.

With that, the man sunk to the ground, almost collapsing down to his knees, his hands covering his face.

Sun heard a quiet reply. It was a soft voice, broken and spiritless. "Home."

Sun asked him in her mind again, this time something different. "Train?" The question just seemed to come out of her.

She heard a frantic reply: "Train. Dogs. Men. Men! Men!"

"Hide," Sun said, and with that, the man vanished. He didn't run, he didn't cease to exist, he just began to … slow down … to someplace else until he was gone.

Sun stood, her hands trembling. She wasn't really scared, but at the same time, she felt as if she had just stepped into a world that, by scale, made her feel as small as a grain of sand.

Somewhere in the distance, she thought she heard a train whistle, lifting quietly, slowly, until it faded without ever truly being heard.

As Sun turned back in the direction of the house, she was met with Nellie's muzzle.

"Red eyes." The words came through as clearly from Nellie as if she had spoken them out loud herself.

Sun was perplexed and then thought of the canal, the train bridge, the hole, the photo of the Waxman Flyer, and the field missing its rabbits.

"Hole?" Sun asked.

"Home."

THE RANGE

Sun thought long and hard about what the gray man had said. She wasn't sure what it all meant, but her experience with animals and her long life in the area helped fill in her thoughts.

The train, the horse, the canal, the sound of the whistle—all of it seemed to say something.

It was the kind of feeling she had when she talked to animals that had never known a person could communicate clearly with them. The first time, they were always startled.

Hole. Home. There was something there too, she pondered. *The train whistle. The train passing. The fear. The running. The violence.*

Sun went to the town doctor's office to talk to him. He was an old country doctor. His family had been around for generations, and if he had seen as many strange things in his life as she had experienced in hers, maybe he could help.

He was in his office writing out some reports when she knocked.

"Hello there, Dr. Sun. Come on in. Just finishing up. Fancy some coffee? How's that badger you saved a few weeks ago? Let it loose yet?"

She laughed. "Tried to, but she likes my cats so much she won't leave. She's living under the back porch now, and she's nursing some kittens for me. Sleeps with them at night."

"Well, I'll be. I thought I'd heard them all. Saw a dog nurse fox pups once. Saw a parakeet raise some bat babies too. Never knew they could do that."

"Doc, you've been here a long time. What's your take on all this?" Sun's face was calm but far away, almost scared. She knew what he was going to say. She didn't want to hear it, but she knew she would. As she waited for the words to come, she looked at the photograph of the Waxman locomotive on the wall.

"I've been raising and caring for folks around here for, well, longer than you've been living. Longer than even that, I guess. This land's alive. It's got secrets. It's got life. Never been any place like this ever that I know of. This place just seems to be boiling with things that come from someplace else in the world, or things beyond it."

Sun thought about that for a moment. "But all these deaths, all these killings … now Cal's gone. Murdered. Who's doing this? What's doing this?"

The doctor took a long, deep breath, leaned way back in his chair, and interlaced his fingers. Then he propped up his shin on his hands before beginning to speak. "The war. The Civil War … not a good name for it. That war changed so many things. I remember my own grandfather telling me stories about the walking wounded, straggling up and down the Blood Trail, trying to get home. Both sides out of powder, out of food, and out of hope. They left each other alone just so they could make it one more step. It was a time of butchery that we weren't prepared to endure here. It ruined this country. We'd barely been free of it eighty years, and we were back into it again. It's come back home. The killing, I mean. Lincoln was wrong. He should have let the South go and then reformed it through treaties and diplomacy. Who knows where we'd be now as a country. A lot less dead, a lot less pain. So much pain. Whole family lines wiped out. And so many lost souls, wandering—"

"Wandering souls," she said to herself.

The vet sat still, thinking. Something about that made sense, or at least it was important. As she thought of this, she also thought of the face of the gray man.

"You know, before the sheriff rode out there, he asked me to hold on to something for him." The doctor pulled back the center drawer of his desk and took out a small leather pouch. "He told me this was the key, the thing that would make all the sense to the right person. I don't know… maybe to you."

The doctor handed her the pouch.

She opened the pouch and held the gold watch and a small piece of paper in her hands. Something else was wrapped up in a piece of cloth. As she looked at the items, a small photograph of the Waxman locomotive seemed to come unhinged from the wall and hit the floor with a crash.

She jumped, but the doctor was steady. He stood up quietly, retrieved the photograph, and set it aside. Without saying a word, the doctor smiled, nodded to her, and walked down the hall to the rear of the office and then out into the field.

Sun got the overwhelming sense that something very important had just happened. A message had come through. She tried hard to pay attention, hoping she could catch it and make sense of the time and place she was in.

She slipped her nail into the small slit in the gold rear cover of the watch and popped it open. The two photographs stared back at her, and briefly, for a moment, she failed to recognize them, like they were blurred. And then, slowly, they became clear to her.

"Sometimes," she heard the doctor's voice say from outside, "things have to run their course and just wait for the right person to bring them home." The voice faded.

With that, she heard a car start and drive away.

THE DARK

T HE TIME FINALLY CAME that Sun had known was going to come. She wasn't scared, wasn't afraid. She just felt in her soul that it was time to set things right and to make the world a place of peace, if only in her own way and in her own sphere of living. There was a snag in the fabric of life, and it was time to find it and smooth it out.

She drove out to the canal alone. It was very late afternoon, and the sidelight of the day made the whole landscape look like a painting she had seen in a museum while away at school—quiet, deep shadows, the texture of the light and the earth together looking like a place of privacy and reservation. It was a landscape that spoke of civility, of morality, but with a hidden element of uncertainty and unpredictability to it and the potential for harshness if left ignored.

Sun parked along the road, the same place she had the day she'd responded out there to get Nellie. She left the truck and wandered down to the spot where she'd heard Vern Thompson say that the rabbits had all been hunted out.

In her mind, she could see that day, that scene, and she could see the spot where Nellie had frozen in place after running away from the attack.

Sun walked down toward the canal and stood there. The light was beginning to bend around the curve of the earth. The railroad tracks seemed to have little lights jumping on them as the sun shown off of them, and for the first time she could remember, the canal water was moving very slowly, making almost no noise. It was almost like a soft whisper.

And then she turned and looked the way Nellie had been looking that afternoon.

Across the road, way back the other direction, there was a thicket. It was a dark patch, almost like a mound. It was overgrown, a bundle of thorny bushes, but it was very low and small.

Sun moved closer to the road a few steps and lost sight of it. She stopped and squinted, but she couldn't see it. So she backed up to where she had been before.

There it was.

She picked her bearings and then crossed the road, walking slowly, directly toward the thicket. Several times she thought she could see it; other times as she looked, the entire field was flat and barren and empty. The place was almost playing with her, like it was willing to reveal something to her but then quickly changed its mind.

Finally, after a longer walk than she had been expecting, she came to the mouth of the thicket.

The sun behind her was slowly setting. This was the time of the day her mother had told her about, when all things were possible. This was the time when the world might reveal its secrets, or create new ones, and the smallest thing could become a missing key to a mystery far off in the future.

She'd brought her gloves. She rolled her sleeves down on her shirt and pulled the thorny branches covering the mouth of the thicket apart. There was a hole there big enough for an animal, or even a man.

Sun stopped for a minute and thought through the situation. *Bear? No, they preferred the woods with places they could climb. Puma? No, probably not. No livestock attacks, although they could survive on small fowl and other animals easily. They just can't resist the livestock. Badger?* She smiled. *Too big.*

Sun crouched down onto all fours and then shuffled into the hole. She could see. There was still enough light coming through that she could see the inside. Off on the far side of the hole, she could see a snake resting. It was very big, but it was just a black snake, not poisonous. She relaxed. It would have eaten anything else in there that might want to bite her.

"Smooth," the vet said. The snake held itself still for a moment and then slithered silently off, deeper into the thicket.

She sat for a few minutes, smelling the air, feeling the ground. As she sat, her eyes slowly began to see other things there—a campfire ring, a small pile of kindling, a small mound of fiber that looked like it had been a blanket at one time, now stale and disintegrated.

Sun sifted through some dirt with her hands. It felt coarse, sandy, gritty.

What is this place? she thought to herself.

A voice answered her. "Hole." The words jolted her nearly out of her skin.

Sun turned sharply to see the gray man crouching beside the front of the thicket, so close he could have touched her.

"What?"

"Hole." The voice was gruff, dry, almost dusty in its resonance.

Sun was trembling, but she steadied herself.

"Sara." She spoke the name. It was hers as well, but that wasn't what she meant.

The gray man's eyes went wild. They became burning balls of fire. They grew so large they seemed to overwhelm the small thicket, as if it was going to burst into flames.

"Sara!" The voice screamed.

"Sara," she said softly, calmly. "Sara."

The eyes subsided, and then the gray man was there again, this time his head hanging low, his eyes turned down.

"Home." She spoke out loud.

The man's head turned up to hers. "Home." The man's voice tapered off.

Sun's mind flashed back to her grandmother's house, to a set of portraits that had hung above the fireplace. The face of the man in the portrait was in front of her.

"Home. Jack."

The man's face lifted quickly. "Jack," he said. "Jack. My name."

"Home, Grandpa Jack. It's time to get home."

The last light of the day seemed to spill over the horizon just at that moment, and Sun saw that green flash of light, that magical snap of light coming from another place. Jack faded from view, and Sun suddenly felt very tired.

With that, the vet slipped down onto her side, curled up, and quickly fell asleep.

THE NIGHT

S UN AWOKE TO THE sound of dogs and men on horseback. She thought for a moment that maybe the sheriff's posse had come out to look for her. She was about to call out when a hand touched her arm.

The gray man was there next to her. He held his hand up to his face and placed a finger over his lips. She could see him clearly even though it was pitch-black outside. Then he pointed to the opening in the hole, looking out into the field.

The scene was otherworldly, as men on horseback led along groups of soldiers, some of them chained and some of them bound together with rope, across the canal to the rail line. They cast huge shadows in the light of the campfires. Sun instantly grew fearful for the fate of the prisoners, sensing that they were about to meet a diabolical and senseless end.

The sensation that gripped the vet was one of sheer terror. Her heart was pounding so loudly she was sure the men outside would hear it.

There was the sound of a crackling fire burning someplace nearby and the sound of men moaning. And then there was the sound of men screaming and a gun shot and then laughter.

Sun jumped as the sound of the shot rumbled through the thicket. The sound of men laughing came to her as well. She sensed men playing cards, men drinking, and men dying there too.

Through this, she had held in her a sense of anticipation, a sense of fear, and a sense that there was only a single chance to get home.

Home.

Home.

Sun stayed completely still for a long time, maybe hours. She dozed off. Later, she awoke again and listened hard. There were no sounds outside, and the gray man was gone. It was still pitch-black, but a few stars shown through the top of the thicket.

And in her thoughts came the voice of an old woman, a voice she thought she recognized, saying that tomorrow was the day. The Waxman was coming … tomorrow, one last time, and the voice said to wait for the sound of the whistle.

THE LIGHT

S UN STOOD ALONG THE canal, looking down the tracks, the gold watch in her hand. The photographs of the soldier and his wife were there on the open flap, looking back at her. Her family.

She watched the horizon for a long time. Then, seeing a plume of smoke, she put the gold whistle to her lips and slowly, gently, blew it.

The sound lifted quietly at first and then built until it held the shrillness of a steam whistle. She blew it until she knew she could stop. When she did, the world seemed to take on a brightness that was strangely familiar, just like the night she was born. It was like a space had been opened up in the world just long enough to allow for something urgent, necessary, needed, to play itself out.

Just then, the sun broke over the eastern tree line, and the sound of the locomotive was deafening.

The gray man was beside her, his eyes suddenly glistening, shining like the stars had through the thicket that night. Hopelessness, pain, fear, and a longing to get home all shown in his face. He was younger now, but the sense of anguish and pain she got from him was overwhelming. He was a man with only one chance left and no strength left beyond that.

The train approached. As it got closer and closer, she could also hear the sound of barking dogs and galloping horses coming up behind her.

The sound of the train bore down on her.

Just then, the sunlight flashed onto the train bridge and seemed to beam through the opening under the bridge in a way that was almost surreal, like a pathway leading into time.

The gray man was up and running down the tracks, sprinting, gasping, reaching.

"Sara!" he shouted. "Sara!" His arms and legs churned wildly, and he pushed with everything he had. The train started to slip away from him, but he refused to stop.

And with that, the train seemed to slow, just a bit, and he jumped for the rail of the last car, straining, giving every bit of strength, reaching beyond himself to the sound of men cheering and shouting.

He reached, missed, and then reached again, nearly diving headfirst as he grabbed the handrail.

He had made it.

He pulled himself up onboard as the hands and arms of other men onboard reached out to help him. They patted him on the shoulders and hugged him, and Sun could see many faces smiling and laughing. The faces shined back at her, like faces held in time in photographs from days long past.

Jack had made it.

He stood in the open doorway of the railcar looking back to her, and in his eyes, welling with tears, Sun could see that he knew he had made it. He was safe, and he was going home.

Home.

He raised his hand to her and nodded. She could see him mouth the words "thank you." Brilliant light beamed out of the railcar like a sun boring out across the field.

"Home," she heard Jack say. "Sara. Home."

The bright light dancing through the tunnel began to fade. At the same time, Sun felt the sense that the murders, the killings, had ended. She turned around to see the figures of two men on horseback, hounds lying alongside the horses in the dirt.

"We wanna get that one?" one of them said.

"Nah. Let's let that one go. Been a long time hunting him. It's time he got on his way. Us too, I reckon." Then they faded from view, the sound of the dogs dwindling as the light around them became brighter.

As Sun looked down the tracks, the train made the switch onto the line beyond the trees, and the plume faded. She looked at the photographs in the watch and then slowly, quietly snapped it shut. She looked at the gold whistle, a trainman's whistle, and then tucked it into her shirt pocket. That glowing place in the world, the magical moment, had finished.

Sun walked slowly back through the field to her truck and drove home. She didn't hear a single sound the whole way. It was as if the world had finally exhaled and was, for just a moment, at rest. There was no need for sound now. The world was simply being.

And once there at home, on the mantle where all of her other family heirlooms rested, she hung the watch in a glass dome alongside the photographs of the soldier and his wife and placed the whistle in a small wooden box. When she was done, she took Nellie for a long, quiet walk.

Much later, while out riding along that canal, Sun saw a family of rabbits out along the water, drinking. And with them was a new brood of bunnies playing. Off in the distance she saw a family of grouse scrambling around and feeding on bugs.

"Home," she heard Nellie say. "Home."

Home.

THE PEACE

Sun's own daughter played in the big bedroom alongside the heirlooms of the family but was careful to not touch anything.

"Momma, what's this?" she asked, pointing to the glass dome with the watch.

"Sara, you know who that is. That's Grandpa Jack and Grandma Sara."

"Well, I know that," she said smartly. "I mean this." Little Sara pointed to the wooden box.

"That's the whistle."

"Did you ever blow it?" the girl asked.

"I did, just once. You hadn't been born yet, but you were on the way."

The girl fidgeted. "And why do we call Grandpa Jack *grandpa*? He's really older than that."

"He is. He's really my Great-Grandpa Jack. He's my mother's granddad."

"And Grandma Sara, she's really Great-Grandma Sara?"

Sun put down her book, went over to the bed, and lifted her daughter up onto her lap.

"Yes, that's right. She's really my Great-Grandma Sara."

"And so that makes me which Sara?" The girl giggled.

"That makes you the newest Sara." Sun tickled her, and she squirmed.

They hugged, and then little Sara jumped up and bounded down the stairs.

"I'm going to play!" she called as she bashed through the screen door onto the porch.

"Take Blue with you."

The dog heard his name and ran after her.

Sun sat on the bed and rested her hand on the wooden box, looking at the photographs of Jack and Sara. They somehow looked content but stern at the same time, the way reserved, rural folks did in old photographs. There was dignity there and pride and a sense of respect for what the world was.

The whistle rested in the box, polished, brilliant, and very quiet.

And for a moment, Sun felt a wave of relief that something very important had finally been settled. At the same time, she had a sense that there was far more to be done before she was through.

A voice rose up from downstairs. It was her husband. "Sun, I'm going over to the McMahans' place. They just called; they think they have a breach birth starting in the barn."

"Need help?" she called back.

"No, I can do it. You enjoy the afternoon. I'll be back later."

She could hear her daughter running down the trail toward the back woods, with Blue jumping and running alongside. At that moment, she saw the sun crack through the trees. And she also heard the sound of a truck engine starting up, and then the quiet rumbling of the truck as it made its way down the long drive to the main road.

Far off in the distance, Sun heard the sound of a train whistle lifting above the sounds around her, lessening quietly until it had faded with the light.

That evening, as Sun sat on the front porch waiting for little Sara and Blue to finish their chores in the barn, she looked up the path to the fence that surrounded the house. Standing alongside the gate was a pair of gray wisps of what seemed like water vapor, and as Sun lifted herself off of the chair on the porch and looked more closely, she thought she saw a couple, a man and a woman, standing quietly, looking back at the house.

The man was dressed in a well-tailored riding suit with tall leather boots and a waistcoat, and the woman had on a fine lace gown. They looked peaceful, reserved, proud, almost dignified, the way old Southern gentlepeople did. They looked her way for a moment and then turned away slowly and strode arm in arm down the lane, toward the wooded glen.

Just then, little Sara and the dog bounded up the back porch steps, through the long open foyer, and onto the front porch.

"Momma, we're home!"

The girl jumped into Sun's chair. The dog yelped as the little girl began rocking back and forth.

"Home."

Home.

PART TWO

THE GRAY

Time passed gently. Little Sara grew, the farm flourished, and Sun and her husband seemed to finally reach that place in life where things felt settled.

Being a family of veterinarians in a rural community made for times that were measured by the birth of new life and the passing of old life. In between were the emergencies, the tragedies, and the challenges of reconciling life's ways. Sun knew that this was true life; her husband knew it, and little Sara knew it as well. Life was like the seasons.

Her daughter had grown increasingly attached to Nellie, and as a parent, Sun was very proud of her for jumping headlong into caring for animals. But as a veterinarian, Sun also knew that Nellie was getting older and slower and would eventually be gone. She worried that this might be the one childhood love that would, upon Nellie's leaving, shatter Sara's heart and render Sun nearly powerless to guide her daughter through the loss. It would be a loss for her too. It was the way of life, undeniable, yet inevitable. There was nothing she could do to change it. But for the time being, Sun was proud.

Nellie would follow Sara all the way to the end of the road in the morning and would later wait for her to return home from school. They had a magical kind of friendship. Although Sun never asked her if she could hear Nellie talk, she knew she could.

One day late in autumn, Nellie didn't appear at the end of the road to greet Sara, now almost in her teens. Sara ran all the way to the house worried that something had happened to her. When Sara got there, she saw her mother and father sitting alongside Nellie, who was lying on her side in the front yard by the gate.

"Mom? Is she okay? What's wrong? Dad?" Sara was almost in a panic but held herself in check. She'd seen enough of the cycle of life and death to know that some things just happened.

Nellie heard Sara's voice, lifted her head to look, and then laid it back down, seemingly succumbing to sheer exhaustion.

"She's tired." Sun rubbed Nellie's face, running her hand over the horse's neck. "She's a tired girl. It's been a long life."

Sun had given the horse a thorough checking over and couldn't find anything except that old wound on the ankle, which seemed to have gotten strained and had swollen up a bit. As Sun ran her hand along the scar that covered the entire length of Nellie's back, Nellie instantly tried to stand. She struggled a bit but finally righted herself and walked over to the gate. Looking toward the open field, she stood there, almost frozen in time.

Sun felt a cold, almost harsh, pain in her stomach.

It's Jack. It's Grandpa Jack. Something's wrong, Sun said to herself.

With that, Nellie heard her speaking. She brayed like a mule for a moment and then turned her gaze back to the field.

There was something going on, sometime in the past.

Something *bad.*

THE ESCAPE

WHEN JACK HAD RESCUED Nellie from the snare she had gotten caught in, he had hoped that letting her loose might distract the skinners from his scent. She had trotted off through the woods and across a few miles of scrub, the wet rag tied around her ankle. It eventually came loose and wound up tossed into a patch of briar, up high enough from the ground to catch the breeze. The light scent drifted for miles, and just as Jack had hoped, it had caught the nose of the hounds and steered the skinners away from him.

Nellie hadn't been so lucky. She was finally got caught by some Union wranglers and led into a fenced corral with other horses. Her ankle had bled sufficiently to cause her to look like she had a red boot on one leg. One of the kids the Union had brought in to feed and handle the horses noticed it and had approached her to check on it.

"Nasty cut there," he said to one of his friends. "Let's see if I can take a look."

Nellie tolerated the young handler's touch, and he was eventually able to wipe away the blood and pack the wound with some roots and tree sap. "We'll put this one in the side stall for a bit, maybe help her to heal up. She's a big horse. Wouldn't want to lose her to an infection."

Nellie heard the other horses calling to her, but there was nothing she could do but wait.

THE CALL

S UN STOOD OUT ALONG the outer fence of the house, watching as the sun began to slope slowly out along the horizon. The light started to begin to bend, the shadows seemed to come alive for just a minute or so, and everything had the radiance of that old painting she remembered from school. The moment was so alive that she could almost feel the light breeze coming from the rays of the sun.

She looked about, making sure that Tom really had taken Sara on a walk out along the farthest pastures of the farm and she was alone. She felt foolish at first, and then the memories of her experience with Jack snapped her back in to the moment. This was real, this was actually happening, and she needed to finally admit it to herself. The world was a larger place than simple faith could explain away. And life was something that was alive; it moved, and it grew. And sometimes it called out.

She held the gold whistle in her hand, rolling it back and forth, thinking. And then, carefully, she lifted it to her lips and blew it, steadily and for as long as she could. The sound raised itself over the land, and for a moment, the sun in the low sky paused its travel, as if it was being held there by the clouds beneath it.

The light shifted in front of her, imperceptibly, and the wind was making the rose bushes along the fence shudder just a bit. But the shuddering didn't stop. In front of Sun, a thin mist of dark air seemed to come together and then elongate upward until it took the form of a face she knew. The face held itself in place for just an instant, and then its features and details came into focus and the entire body took shape.

It was Grandpa Jack. He had come, just as she had known he would.

"Jack." Sun's voice was firm, but fearful.

"Sun. I see you." He hovered forward just enough to place a hand on her arm, a friendly gesture. Sun could feel his touch; it was warm and comforting.

"Jack, it's Nellie. She's in pain."

"Nellie." Jack's eyes seemed to transform, as if they were looking far away, and then they came back to look at Sun's face.

Jack's voice became hollow, almost disembodied. "Bad things. Bad things. Nellie's in trouble—she needs. She needs." Jack's words were detached from Sun's world, disjointed and confused. It took a moment for Jack to orient himself. His face held a scowl and then slowly became sad. His speech was stifled. He seemed to be locked in a place of old memories, unable to slip free.

Sun looked at Jack, and she could suddenly see the resemblance to her own daughter. She reached out and touched his arm. Jack smiled.

"What can I do?" Sun's voice was patient but urgent.

"Save her. Save little Nellie. You can cross over."

Little Nellie? Sun wondered. She didn't understand.

"You can cross over. I'll show you." Jack's eyes were blazing hot, intense. And yet, through that, Sun could sense the kindness and empathy of the man standing there.

Sun didn't know what to say, but her nerves were steady.

"You can cross over." His voice was calmer now, clear. His eyes focused on her.

Sun nodded her head. There wasn't any point in delaying or arguing with herself. She was standing on the brink of something extraordinary, even beyond the realization that her long-dead grandfather was standing in front of her. There were larger notions dangling from the last few droplets of sunlight, and she knew that there was nothing left to accept other than the new world.

Jack drew his own pocket watch from his vest and carefully slid the winding stem out of place. Sun could see the small second hand on the face come to a stop.

And as Blue sat alongside them watching patiently, Sun and Jack seemed to slow down, quietly, gradually, until the only thing left behind was the golden whistle, sitting on the fence rail.

With that, the sun slipped below the treetops.

Blue unseated himself and yelped a bit as he ran around the fence line.

Just then, Tom and Sara came back from their hike. They entered the house at the back door, went through the main hallway, and ended up out on the front porch. Little Sara stood there for a minute before letting go of her father's hand and running first to the fence where Sun had been and then to the barn. Blue ran with her.

She didn't say a word out loud, but Tom heard her talking to Nellie, who was lying on her side in a stall in the barn.

Tom surveyed the area; not seeing his wife, he got the sense that something had happened. He looked about and sported the gold whistle on the fence post. He took it and placed it in his pocket.

He set himself down on one of the rockers on the porch and waited. Although he was not quite certain what was going on, at the same time, he knew that it was probably better not to interfere.

THE PASSAGEWAY

S UN HEARD A SHRILL sound in her ears and felt as if she was being buffeted around in a windstorm. She could hear voices and noises all about her—coming toward her, passing her, overtaking her. Her field of vision was filled with kaleidoscopic images, things that seemed to be jumbled all together, interwoven, intertwined like a mosaic of memories and sensations.

Ahead of her, she thought she could see Jack leading her through what felt like a swirling, shaking hallway into another room of a house she felt she recognized but couldn't describe. She felt her skin tightening, almost to the point of being brittle, the way skin looked in old photographs. And then she felt her face growing very hot, and just then, she found herself standing along an old broken fence line with a dilapidated house overgrown with scrub behind her.

The air was absolutely silent, as if it had been vibrating all around her and had suddenly frozen in place. She took a breath of air, feeling very insignificant, very small, like a leaf that had just been blown across entire worlds. And with that sensation, she felt her feet underneath her, as if she had just been grounded like a live wire.

There on the ground next to her was a railroad oil lantern, turned way down low, which glowed quietly. Next to it she saw a pair of boots, finely polished, almost glimmering in the soft light.

"We're here." Jack's voice resonated for just an instant.

Sun lifted her gaze higher to see Jack, clearly and plainly, for the first time. His voice was free of its unnatural restrictions in the other place.

He was a handsome man. He stood with dignity, with poise, and with spirit, and his body language transmitted confidence, but with discretion. His clothes were perfect, not a thread out of place.

But Sun couldn't tell if he was in uniform or in civilian clothes; the distinctions were hard to make. Even though she couldn't tell exactly

119

what he was wearing, she could easily make out a cavalry officer's saber, and a holstered cap-and-ball pistol slung crossways on his belt. Above it in his vest was a gold watch chain, laced through a button hole between pockets. It seemed to almost glow red, like hot metal.

"Where are we?" She hesitated and looked around her. "Wait … I know this place." Sun's face was bright with hope. She looked about, and as her eyes made their way across the front of the house, it began to change, to straighten, to grow, until it was so brilliant and so beautiful that she could barely take in all of its detail. And as she looked more, she began to see people there, faces whose names she instantly knew.

"This is the place in between. This is home. You recognize it? It's your home too." Jack's voice was now clear, deep, and reassuring.

And as she ran her eyes along the front of the house, she caught a glimpse of a shiny patch of air standing out back by the exercise ring. She couldn't make out what it was, but the shape seemed to jump and dance about and then stop.

Sun was overwhelmed. On the porch, rocking gently with needlepoint on her lap, was Great-Grandma Sara, and alongside her resting on its haunches was Blue. Standing next to her, along the wall of the porch, was Vern Thompson's grandfather, and next to him was Old Man Waxman. They disengaged from their conversation to greet her eyes, and Sun felt a welling up of emotion. Others were nearby as well, faces she had seen in old photographs as a little girl. All of them were now gentle, quiet souls. They nodded.

"We'll stop here for a rest, and then I'll take you all the way there."

"There's more?" Sun's voice strained for just a bit. Sun suddenly felt scared. Not the kind of fear an adult feels, but the kind of fear she felt as a little girl during a nightmare. Her stomach went numb. The feeling gripped her like a vise.

Jack's voice grew dark. "There's the bad part left to go."

THE WALK

T HE NEXT PART HAPPENED without Sun realizing it had started. There was the sound of wings flapping, beating hard, like a bird trying to get off the ground. Next came the growing sound of a screech, like something building up toward a massive explosion that subsided at the last instant. Then there was the sensation of bone-chilling cold, and a wave of sorrow came over her. Images passed in front of her eyes too quickly for her to really see them, but the emotions associated with them struck her like a thousand blows to the heart.

And then she was there.

It was a full moon. Sun found herself laying face down in a field, and the smell of straw and freshly turned soil was strong in her nose.

It was very still.

The sound of cannon fire jarred her back into awareness that she was now very much present in a place sometime in the past. The sounds were clear and crisp, and they insisted on her attention. The surrounding fields and tree lines waltzed about like gentle specters as streams of cannonballs streaked downward, followed by the echoes of explosions and the screams of men torn apart. Across the field ahead of her she could see small clusters of soldiers lying flat against the earth, surrounded by burning spots where cannonballs had erupted, sending dirt and stone and flesh skyward.

Jack was beside her, crouching low, lifting himself up enough to get a view of the battlefield without attracting attention. He was now clearly in his Confederate uniform, his pistol in hand and his hat slung low on his head.

Sun felt the need to cry, but Jack put his hand over her mouth and instructed her not to make a sound.

They waited a long time.

Finally, Jack nodded to her.

"Is this … is this the war?" Sara whispered.

"It's like it but not the war you know. It's another war where things happen out of time. Here, all kinds of things happen that history never knows. When you die here, your soul never escapes. People fight and die and are resurrected to fight again. It never ends."

Sun looked about, but her attention was brought back when she heard the sound of a rifle ball whizzing past her head. Jack instinctively rolled himself flat and then, taking her hand, led Sun away from the field.

They instantly were somewhere else. Now it was daytime, and they found themselves standing alongside a trail that was glimmering red in the sun. It was the Blood Trail.

Sun saw endless lines of men moving past her coming from each direction, sullen, starving, desperate, bloodied. Their faces were obscured by their caps and hats or by bandages wrapped over their faces, their wounds open and streaming.

"Who are they?" Sun asked as she felt the men brush past her.

"They're the ones who'll never make it home—lost, no one to know them." Jack's face was solemn, his gaze looking farther away. "They've got nowhere to go and no way to get there. They'll be marching here forever."

"But look at them. They're almost dead." Her eyes were wide now, searching for something she could latch onto to anchor herself, but the sight had overwhelmed her sense of reality. The full weight of her circumstances was becoming clear to her. This was a very dangerous place, a place where people should never go to if they had a choice. This was a place where irreversible things could happen, changing time and life forever.

Suddenly, Jack and Sun were swept away to another place, this time to a battlefield where mounds of men lay, their uniforms soiled and rotting, as far as the eye could see.

"Jack, why are we here? What can I do?" Sun tried to stay focused on Jack, but he was slowly slipping away.

"Little Nellie. Her mom's nearing a bad end. Got to find her and get her back to the other place, or she may never be." Jack hesitated. "We … we don't have much time."

Time? What is time here? Sun thought. *Is there time? Is there my time?*

Sun let the notion sink in. She realized that Jack couldn't defy time and tell her exactly what she needed to know, but the words were starting to make sense nonetheless.

Sun had a job to do, a patient to care for, and she had to do it as soon as she could.

She straightened herself. "Let's go."

THE BUTCHERS

THE RING OF HORSES was tight to keep them from getting away. Alongside the ring was a line of wooden frames that stretched far off into the field and long into the distance. Hanging on the frames were the bodies of horses that had been butchered, some still twitching.

The horses in the ring knew their fate. They were restless and terrified. The men butchering them didn't shoot them. They hung them upside down and slit their throats to drain the blood from them. The cries of the dying horses stirred even more anxiety in those waiting their turn. The soullessness of the act rested beyond the furthest reach of comprehension, and as each horse died, the men seemed to consume their being.

The air was filled with the stench of blood, of rotting meat, and of debilitating fear. And slowly, methodically, the butchers went about their work. The eyes of the butchers were dark and hollow, nearly empty. They weren't doing what they did for survival. This was not a place where hunger could ever be satisfied. They did what they did because they gained the power of existence over living things and indulged their thirst for suffering.

They weren't even men or the old spirits of men, not anymore. They were the workers of all things dark—of pain, of hatred, of death. They were the flesh feeders, the stealers of light, and the cheaters of the wheel. This was their place in this existence, in all existence, a place of suffering and of sorrow and of the growing hatred for life, the thing they themselves had been denied.

They thrived on the moment of surrender and collapse and of bringing that moment back again and again. These men were things that existed in the gaps of reality, where suffering was only one of many torments. There was no gratification, no lust. It was sheer consumption of existence into darkness.

And somewhere in the ring of horses, all trembling and slowly dying of thirst, stood Nellie, her leg festering and slowly turning gangrenous. Inside of her slept an unborn offspring struggling to join the world.

Somewhere else, beyond the reaches of shadowy time, little Sara lay next to her Nellie in the barn, watching her slowly dwindle away and listening to the heartbeat of her unborn colt, barely hearing its voice.

THE HOLLOW

JACK LED SUN TO a narrow ravine, covered by old scrub oaks overgrown like a briar thicket. They made their way through it carefully. Sun saw snakes all around, but as she tread, the snakes quickly slithered away from her. They walked farther and farther into the shadows until they came to a campfire in the middle of small, rocky gorge. Around the fire were several men, all huddling next to each other. Behind them stood a huge old tree, almost entirely entwined in its own roots and branches.

Sun raised her hand to the fire and couldn't feel any heat. It was as if it was merely for show. Even the light from the fire seemed almost illusionary. And Sun couldn't tell what time of day it was; it was as if it was no time at all.

Jack motioned to her to step forward. As she did so, the faces of the men around the fire brightened, and she could see their features clearly. They were young faces, hopeful and ambitious, and they smiled and spoke to her. They were lost men, forlorn and abandoned to time. But Sun's presence was giving them life. As she watched, their appearances shifted, as they had within the other place she had visited, from old to new.

"I'm Sun. Who are you all?"

The men only smiled and nodded politely, some of them exchanging quiet words between them.

"They can't speak. They're afraid the skinners might find them. After a while, they can't talk at all, at least not loud enough for you to hear. Lots of men from many wars become like that. They lose their voices." Jack took his place by the fire. "But I can talk for them."

"What do I need to do? I have to know." Her words made the fire glow hotter.

"I can't tell you that. I can only help you. You have to tell me." Jack's eyes were furious now, almost brimming over with fire.

Sun swallowed hard. "I—" she began, "I need to find Nellie and bring her home. Will you help me?" She looked at the faces around the fire, all of whom looked far away. Slowly, they nodded.

"Are there enemies here? Things that could hurt you?" she asked.

The men were reluctant to tell her, but Jack reassured them that it was necessary. One of the men, a thin, almost gaunt horse soldier, spoke quietly. His eyes were hollow, and his wrists so thin that they looked like sticks.

"There're bad men out there," was all he could say. "They're killing everything that comes their way." The man's voice trembled. "Man is butchering life just to see it suffer."

Sun looked more closely at the man. His voice sounded familiar, but the shadows and the darting glare of the fire seemed to hide him from her.

She could see memories in the flames of the fire, images of things. The horror, the cruelty, and the suffering were immense, so much so that she felt the weight of the world pressing on her chest. She felt tears welling up in her eyes but fought the sensation. The men around the fire looked on, and she drew a strange sense of empathy coming from them, as if they too had all been in exactly the same place, over and over again, for an infinite amount of time.

But she felt a resolve as well, something that welled up in her to face the realization that in this place, made up of all the life she stood within and among, any misstep would be lethal. This would be the place where instinct and the rightness of truth would do battle with all things dark, loathsome, and despised. Sun realized that everything she was, and everything that would ever be beyond her, was coming down to this place, this moment.

"Then let's go," Sun announced. "Let's get Nellie and anything else still alive, and let's end this."

As Sun stood up, the light of the fire bathed her in white light. Suddenly, a beacon of light shot up from the ground where she stood, high above into the sky, and a massive sound began to build around her. It started out like a low, quiet drumbeat that transformed into a flute, and then a crying violin, and then built and built into a crescendo of horns until it blared out into the night. As the sound traveled, those things in that reality touched by it turned to solid gold. The light around it became crystalline, like diamonds, dropping to the ground, glistening and sparkling.

The men before her seemed to suddenly grow younger, their clothes mending and straightening. Soon, they were as young and as fit as the best of men could be. Their eyes shined of light and fire, and their faces reflected a strange resolve, as she had felt inside of her.

The best of men, she thought. *For them, this is the place, and this is the time. This is all there is. And the time, for all time, is now.*

Sun lifted her hands to her face and saw in her palms a glow, almost a shimmering, of power and force and will so blinding that she could barely look at them. She felt a strange sensation go up her spine to the top of her head.

"That's the strength. That's what I call it," Jack said. "That's what they're killing for. They feed off of it."

Sun swallowed. "Then let's use it while I've got it in me. Let's go get our girl and lay those things low to death."

She saw the ages of time and living pass right through her. Off on a hillside nearby, Sun saw a line of women, each standing firm and looking hopeful, their eyes shining and their hands bidding her luck. Sun nodded, and her eyes narrowed.

"Let's go. We've got work to do."

The group of men quickly rose from around the fire, gathered their things, and briskly walked off into the night.

The fire died away almost instantly, and the shadows advanced onto the place where they had been, consuming every ounce of light. In an instant, the place was barren, dusty, like an old photograph of a place no one could recognize. The place was gone.

The fight for everything there—for existence, for life, for Nellie, and for the survival of future memory—had just grown intense. And far off, amid a line of horses strung up and bleeding to death from the gaping slashes in their necks, the butchers' eyes began to shine like fire too.

They sensed food—energy, suffering, and death.
Death.
Death was life to them.
They smiled.

THE REMINDER

Back home, little Sara sat with Nellie in the barn as the skies grew suddenly dark. A lone, long lightning bolt streaked across the sky. The accompanying thunderclap sent Sara upright; she frowned just for an instant.

Nellie's eyes grew scared.

"That's Mom." *She's started a fight*, thought Sara.

Nellie peered back, through the pain and the anguish, and Sara reassured her with a wink.

"We're going to get through this … all of us."

Somewhere out there, she knew, her mother was about to put up the fight of a lifetime, of a million lifetimes, for her, for Nellie, and for everything she knew to be true and right.

"It's okay, girl. I'm not going to let anything happen to you or little Nellie." Sara stroked the horse's neck and calmed her down.

Her lips tightened, and Sara's hands grew firm on the horse's mane. And for an instant, Sara thought she felt a light kick come from within the old horse. It was just a reminder, a footnote, that all things were connected and that the fight was for more than just a single life.

It was for all of them—all who had come before and all who would ever come again.

For this fight, little Sara knew she'd have to use the secret she'd never shared, not even with her mom. It was her only way to help, and it was time.

Sara shuddered for a moment. The thought of calling that … thing, that person … forth almost terrified her. Once it was done, once it was loose, there was no putting it away. It would roam until its task was done so that it might sleep again. That was its reward—to sleep.

She rose to her feet, petting Nellie along the muzzle before stepping out of the barn. She ran down to the back clearing, knowing that once she did this, there was no way to undo it.

THE KEEPSAKE

S ARA HAD PLAYED ALL around the expanse of the farm, often going on long walks with Blue out past the furthermost fence post and beyond. She knew of the bank along the river where the train would pass by, and she knew about the place in the clearing where Grandpa Jack used to sit on hot days, trying to see a way home through the waves of heat rising over the land toward the railroad tracks.

And she also knew of another place, a deep ravine with a huge tree hollow, an old tree, where things could … sort of … disappear. It was at this place where she had taken her keepsake. And when she had first seen it, a common item from any farm, she knew immediately what it was and what it could do.

The animals all around the place had been shy of going to that ravine, all except Nellie, who used to lead her there and stand along the ridgeline that led down to the creek bed. Nellie would watch as Sara explored, with Blue patiently tagging along, occasionally barking at a snake or sniffing around a squirrel's nest. But it was clear in Sara's mind's eye that there was something there, like a hole in a fence or a path through thick bushes into a hidden garden. There was a clearing on the other side, a place of soft light and soothing smells, but Sara couldn't quite see it.

And she knew of the man who sat in that garden on the other side. He was a man of long memory, of naked power, of duty, and he was a man of tremendous danger. She couldn't tell how old he was. He had kind eyes and smooth hands, and his voice was quiet and almost too soft. He had a voice that seemed perfect for talking to horses.

But he was a dangerous man.

To step through and talk to him, or to invite him to come and help her, would be full of irreversible risks.

Sara knelt at the base of the old gray tree hollow and slowly,

133

patiently, dug at the base of one of the biggest roots. She pushed aside several small mounds of sandy earth until she felt the end of the keepsake with her fingers. She dug around it and then pulled it from the ground.

She cleared away the crusty earth from the cloth wrapped around it and then held it up in front of her.

A horseshoe.

It wasn't just a plain, old, rusted horseshoe—there were plenty of those scattered around. She had picked it out of a box of horseshoes at the county fair, her dad buying it for her for a penny. The old man at the fair had smiled when she picked it. This one seemed to glow and to resonate. It felt light and heavy at the same time. It made her fingers feel fuzzy. The old man at the fair had winked at her and then turned his back. Sara had been distracted for a moment and looked elsewhere. When she turned back, the old man was gone.

After pulling it from her secret spot, she was very careful to lay it back down on the ground without tipping the open end either up or down. She remembered the story about how horseshoes either caught luck like a bucket if turned upright or let it fall away if turned upside down.

Sara relived in her mind the moment in time when the shoe had been lost, kicked off at full gallop, as the man in the garden had passed through to another place. The shoe had been red-hot and had so scorched the ground that it had melted into it, submerged.

It was a relic from a quest long accepted in the past, or future, she couldn't be sure. But it was a powerful thing.

An owl landed on a nearby tree branch across the ravine and peered at Sara. It hooted quietly, and she looked up the hill to the top of the ridgeline. Wrapping the horseshoe in the folds of her dress and slipping the whole thing into her dress pocket, she lifted herself off of the ground and ran up the hill and back home. Blue ran alongside her, never looking back.

As she passed beyond the ridgeline, back into the fields, the old gray tree hollow seemed to shift just a bit, and the hole she had dug simply filled itself in. The tree literally took a deep breath, and then paused there, holding it patiently.

The insects around the hollow resumed their low noise, and the creek bed where she had just been was now covered with hoof prints, each of them existing for only an instant before disappearing in the light wind that came down into the shadowy ravine, rustling the leaves.

THE HAVEN

Old Man Waxman sat quietly in his wooden chair, leaning back just a bit on the rear legs, looking off into the evening sky. The porch creaked imperceptibly. The sheriff was standing nearby, resting his hands on the porch railing, his hands patiently folded as he leaned onto them.

Both of them could see a vaporous remnant of what looked like a lightning strike somewhere out beyond the rim of their time.

"The girl's started in," the sheriff said quietly.

Waxman just nodded. The sheriff wasn't expecting a reply at all. He knew and accepted the realization that the moment in their time had come. Everything they were, everything they seemed to be now, came down to the bravery of a woman still living in the flesh, an unborn horse, and the judgment of a young girl who held so much power in her hands that all of reality was dangling delicately in the air, like a cobweb.

Their fate was now left to the actions of those long cultivated, long sought, and long planned for, to end a thing that had gone so terribly wrong through the will of Men.

Off along the far rim, the place where worldly things vanished into nothing, both men could see the low embers glowing of the forces that had amassed along the edge of their serene world, waiting patiently to slowly step across into it when the time came. It was their appetite to consume souls—their life force, their memories, their line of ancestors, everything they had ever done—and render them into dust. They were like shadows bending in the night, first seeming like men or animals or even like the apparitions of things long gone to history. In their ripping of flesh, entire realities were consumed. They were the agents of nothingness—the end of existence.

Neither man spoke of it. They only waited patiently for the moment to come when they would either step through to their final place of repose, if it could be called that, or be dragged underground into the caverns of a dark forever.

They had all seen this place in between as they had passed through, and they had no fear of it. They all knew that to go there meant to be stripped of all things—human dignity, compassion, empathy, even sincerity. It was a place where the most base and vile things of life dwelled, a place where the light of inspiration was drained away like blood, like life itself, until all that remained was a memory of an urge to feel the subtle jump of a beating heart beneath the skin.

This was the place where existence, where consciousness, had crawled from, where the first unsteady scream of life had happened, where it had been heard, and where it had submerged time and again over all of existence into the dust of nothingness. There was nothing in that place—no loyalty, no love, no mindfulness of worldly obligation. There was only the feeding of insatiable hunger, of a lust for suffering, and the inevitable surrendering of innocence to dismemberment. All atrocities were indulged there and reenacted over and over again, across the span of forever, with every sensation of revulsion and regret exploited.

It was as if hyenas were greedily digging at the soft underbelly of a freshly born calf, still standing, so beautiful and innocent in its new life, being overcome by the harshness of a world the lessons of which it had yet to learn and now never would. The understanding of the potential of the world would come swiftly to it at the very last moment of consciousness, when total, unqualified fear would grip the soul as it was ripped away and cast into a dark, stinking hole.

Only the trembling of the experience of slaughter would keep it company, now and for all of eternal time.

The sheriff, recently having found his way to the plantation house, still saw memories from his old life. He especially remembered the giant red eyes that had engulfed him the very moment he had passed through. He and Jack and chuckled about that after the sheriff had found his senses and accepted where he was and why he was there. It was the only way Jack could get him on the right side where anything could be done to end the line of what was out of balance.

Once the sheriff had made it, the whole thing made sense. In this place, there was no panic, no emotion. There was only an acknowledgment that time was the one element that mattered.

The two men looked at one another for a moment, the sheriff accepting a pipe's worth of tobacco. He sat down next to Waxman, the chair creaking as his weight settled into it.

"The girl's got some spunk in her," Waxman said softly as he drew on his own pipe. The smell of the burning tobacco was more like incense, like ambrosia, as he drew it in and then calmly let it drift from his mouth.

The sheriff smiled. "Yep, she's always been like that. Jumps in with both feet."

"The kid too. Just like her granddad several times removed."

Waxman twisted his head a bit to take in the sheriff's face. Their eyes met, and they gently acknowledged one another again. The sheriff slowly nodded his head.

The men politely nodded as the oldest Sara, Sun's great-grandmother, passed by with Blue on her heels.

"That dog. Been more trouble than I can remember." It was the old veterinarian, who had been standing nearby them, down below on the grass. All three men nodded.

"No complaining about dogs."

The sheriff recognized the voice. It was his Aunt Tillie. He lifted his eyes to see her, and they exchanged a friendly smile. She nodded as if to say that she would come later to see him. He settled back.

Off on the far rim, the place where the worlds of light and shadow met, a low howling rose up from behind the darkness. It was almost like a moan at first, and then it rose even higher to the pitch of a wail. Someplace, another soul had been caught and was being torn to shreds.

The men heard it but didn't look. There was no need to. They knew the eyes of the dark forces were glowing red, like smoldering molten metal, and that those eyes were looking their way.

Old Man Waxman simply sat, held his pipe gently in his hand, and waited.

And out there, somewhere beyond them all, Sun was stepping right into a burning ring, a cauldron of souls, to free an innocent from the grips of eternal death.

THE CUP

Alva Alicia sat patiently on the porch of her cottage, a place far away from anything, overgrown with vines and creepers. It rested quietly in a garden, surrounded by fine white light, almost bathing in it like a sleeping kitten. In her hands rested a porcelain teacup, partly filled with tea.

She swirled the tea about slowly, watching it as it coated the inside of the cup, blousing its way back down to the bottom.

Her eyes were like fire, raging, furious, erupting, and then returning to a state of low intensity for just an instant as she looked at the tea leaves. She seemed to be locked in time, frozen there, digesting something, unmoving until her daughter came to sit next to her.

She touched the cup to her lips, taking the tea into her mouth and then spitting it back into the cup. She looked at the leaves again.

Nothing was said. There was nothing to say.

THE OLD GATE

SARA STOOD AT THE top of the ridge overlooking the ravine. Blue lay in the dirt nearby, watching. The light of day was just then bending along the skyline, and the shadows of the land were growing longer.

With every step Sara took as she slowly made her way down, she felt ripples of time wash over her. They felt like waves of heat, of sound, of rain, of dry wind. She felt in each of them the sensations of lives past twisting along her skin like vines. Some felt like soft ribbons. Others felt like barbed wire. Each one was almost alone to itself.

She reached the bottom of the ravine, gave the base of the huge old tree hollow a sideways glance, and instead of going to it went in the opposite direction down toward the darker side of the creek bed.

There, hidden in the brush and the overhang of many old trees, was what looked like an old garden trellis, the kind someone might have grown roses on, shaped in the form of a rickety archway. It was out of place. The man she had come to see had placed it there long ago.

As she approached, it seemed to brighten up just a bit, and the shadows of the trees above it subsided.

She stood there a long time, holding the horseshoe in her hands.

Finally, she lifted the horseshoe up in front of her, as if to offer it to a stranger, and she held it there, like a gift.

The space inside the trellis didn't move or glow or shudder. Instead, it slowly shed its density, growing thinner and thinner, until it opened up and she could see through it to the other side, into a garden where the light was bright.

Sara scampered through without hesitating, her skirts flapping behind her, her shoes kicking up dust from the creek bed.

The archway grew back quietly, but now it seemed to hold something behind it, something that didn't belong but was accepted as a visitor for the moment.

Blue sat patiently up on the ridgeline, waiting for her to return, and when she didn't come out, he sat down on his haunches and rested his head on his front paws.

THE GARDEN

T HE GARDEN SMELLED LIKE honeysuckle, like jasmine, like fresh pine, like lavender—so many smells. The blossoms of the plants and shrubs glowed. The sunlight was soothing, although it wasn't coming from anywhere in particular.

Sara wandered through the garden until she came to a stone bench erected in the center of one particular clearing.

A man stood beyond it, his back to her, tending the flowers on a vine that had grown up along the trunk of a tree. He sensed that she was there and turned to see her.

His face was pale, almost white, but as he turned more and revealed himself, it changed, as if to suit her.

"So, you've come. I see you." His voice was gravelly. "Why do you seek me?" His words were brittle, almost as if he was speaking another language. She focused on his words.

Sara held up the horseshoe, grasping it like the handle of a teakettle.

The man took in a sharp breath, as if he was scared.

"It has been a long time since … since that time for me. Many, many lives have passed. Many have ended." The man's face grew suddenly dark, almost intense. His words came forth like a storm. "Why … do … you … seek me?" His voice was ear shattering, like a rolling thunderbolt so close that she could almost see it.

Sara defiantly held the horseshoe firmly in her hand. "I'm here to ask something of you. I need your help. Will you help me?"

Seeing the horseshoe made the man subtly step back, cautiously, fearfully.

The offer was something new to him. The very few who had summoned him in the past hadn't asked; they'd only demanded. He eyed the horseshoe carefully.

"Will you help me?" Sara asked again.

The man began pacing back and forth, and as he did so, the light in the garden dimmed to the point that it was almost gone. He was changing in front of her—his shape, his demeanor, everything about him. His voice was now sharp, and he spoke in a pattern of staccatos.

"What world is this? Is this the world of Men? It's been many lives since I've ridden among Men. Killed them. Enslaved them. Crushed their bones. Why do you come?"

"I know who you are. You're the Horse Man." Sara's voice was quiet but firm, belying her age. "I've come to ask you to do something, and if you help me, I'll see to it that you're never disturbed again."

The man's face brightened, and his posture straightened. He gestured to Sara to sit with him.

Off to the side of the clearing stood a small structure made of stone, and under its roof were many things—tools, mementos, human scalps, even what looked like relics of war … a skull, severed at the neck, occupied a place of prominence. Near it, hanging from a wooden peg, was a long, dark cloak and a hat with a brim so wide and floppy it almost seemed to be wilting.

The man saw Sara looking at his cloak and frowned.

"So … it's him you've come to see. The dark rider. Of all the ones I am, he's the last I would ever suspect you'd come for. It's been forever since he's ridden on the earth, ridden a horse at a gallop. It's been a long time since he's thrown down fire and destruction and trampled blood into the mud of time. It's been—" his voice tapered off, "since that shoe was lost. Why would such a young girl ask this of me?"

Sara could see the bridle and the saddle resting on a wooden rack. She nodded toward them.

"If you do as I say, I'll release you. For all time. I will choose the world, but you will be released." She gently lifted the horseshoe. "You … and him. You can leave this place and never return if you do as I say."

The man was silent.

"Do you agree?" Sara asked.

Finally, the man nodded and quietly spoke. "Yes."

"Then sit and listen to your task," she directed.

With that, the man sat on his stone resting place, with Sara across from him, and he listened as she spoke of the task ahead.

She kept the horseshoe firmly in her hands, away from him.

THE PLAN

S ARA SAT AT THE dinner table, and considered her conversation with the man in the garden while picking at her food. Blue was underneath the table sitting by her feet, waiting for her to sneak him a scrap. She wasn't hungry.

"Sara, eat up. It's getting cold." Tom was firm but understanding.

She couldn't. Instead, she asked permission to take her plate to the barn, where she would sit with Nellie and rub her neck and face to calm her. And Sara would place her hands on Nellie's stomach and feel the warmth of her insides and hope for the joy of feeling a kick from within her.

Tom cleaned up the kitchen, fed Blue a few leftover pieces of chicken, and then went to the porch to sit. There were things going on that he didn't understand but that he knew required his patience, and perhaps a leap of faith.

His wife was gone, not missing but … somewhere else. The best he could do was hold down the fort, keep an eye on Sara, and pray that Nellie would hang on until after whatever was happening was over.

No choice.

Inside his shirt pocket he felt the outline of the whistle. He rose, went inside, and placed it inside the wooden box it had come from for safekeeping.

Then he went to the barn to sit with Sara and watch over Nellie.

Through the barn door, off in the distance, he saw a flash of thin lightning but heard no sound for several moments. Then, the sound seemed to roll along the ground, coming toward him, like a galloping horse.

The sound built and built until it was almost on top of him. Nellie quickly rose to her feet, bayed, and trembled for just an instant.

Tom felt a shudder go through his body. It was as if something cold had ridden right through him. He was knocked almost to the barn floor, feeling overwhelmed.

Something, or someone, had just passed through him on its way to somewhere else.

Sara was frightened for just a moment and then quietly said, "It's him. He's riding. He's going to that place."

Tom looked at her, feeling overwhelmed with uncertainty of what to make of all this. He decided then and there that things were in motion that he shouldn't interfere with. Instead, he knelt back down and checked Nellie's pulse as she lay back down. Noticing that it was stronger and faster than usual, he started checking her over again. As his hands passed over Nellie's belly, he felt a kick.

"So that's what this is all about." Tom went back to the house and made a phone call and then came out with his vet bag to begin his work on Nellie and her newly discovered passenger.

"Did you know about this?" Tom asked Sara. She only frowned in response. "Well, it doesn't matter now. We'll do what we can."

Sara watched her dad work. Holding Nellie's mane in her hand, she stroked her neck as she looked out the barn door toward the sunset. The horseshoe was pushed tightly into her skirt pocket.

And in her mind's eye, Sara could see the flaming hoof prints trailing him as he rode off into the other place.

THE RIDE

T HE AIR TURNED TO steam as the rider passed through the woods, the tracks of the horse smoldering in the dirt. The dark cloak trailed behind him, flapping crazily, and with each flap came a massive crack of thunder. The horse's eyes were wild, practically on fire, its breath like a frantic pant. Its legs churned and dug beneath itself as it took huge leaps across the land, sending trees sprawling and rocks tumbling behind it as it ran. With each stride, the rider and horse accelerated until they simply passed beyond.

With them came disaster, defeat, consumption, and surrender.

The eyes of the rider glowed, his face serene and calm, tucked beneath the brim of his hat, which shielded his face from the oncoming wind.

The rider kept his hands tightly on the reins and crouched low over the body of the horse as they rode through time, through worlds, toward the place where the battle was unfolding.

Lashed to the side of the saddle were a leather scabbard, a long battle standard; a staff in two parts with a broad head point; and a canvas sack, which held something unknown.

The rider smiled wryly.

Loose once again.

Loose forever.

Loose on the lives of Men.

Loose … if the task can be done.

The rider quickened his pace even more as the horse seemed to turn to flame, and in an instant, with a massive screech and a billow of smoke, both the man and the horse had passed through into the other place.

He laughed. The sensation of the passage made him remember many other such trips—trips to do deeds, to do tasks, to hunt.

Steam rose in the spot they had been before they vanished. The flaming tracks of the horse smoldered for a moment and then faded in the dirt.

At that moment, back in the barn, to Tom's surprise and to Sara's grave concern, Nellie stood up again. Her belly, made huge by the growing presence of her unborn colt, seemed to want to burst. Nellie stood powerfully on all fours, her head held high and her eyes defiant. She shuddered as she stood. And with one huge inhale, she let out an ear-shattering scream that sent Blue running from the barn out of sheer fear.

And inside of her, a young new life was struggling to see its way into the light of the world.

THE TREK

THE GROUP OF MEN led Sun to an encampment along a tall outcropping of solid granite overlooking a dark field. The rock was huge, jutting up into the sky, with its jagged points looking like giant daggers. The air was crisp and cold, but Sun didn't really notice it. Instead, she was trying to listen to a voice she thought she could hear. It was faint, like a whisper. She cocked her head slightly, as if to help it come to her.

"I hear something." She looked puzzled.

Jack was beside her, surveying the field beyond. He could see the eyes of the dark mass well off in the distance. There was no fear of exposing their presence there. The mass of flesh-eating things could only consume; they couldn't reason. They only saw a meal of energy, not an enemy or an opponent.

"Voices. I hear them all the time too. Sometimes it's words from the past, from other places, or even from yourself. Don't know." Jack kept his voice low.

Sun paused again, this time holding up her hand, as if to quiet the group. Words hovered there around them, just beyond the range of her hearing. It sounded like a low whistle.

"Don't know. But it sounded like a cry," Sun noted

"The horse ring is close. It's just on the other side of the rock." Jack pointed with his pistol. "We'll creep around it, and you'll see."

Sun swallowed hard. She knew what there was to see … things she didn't want to see, things that would tear at the fabric of her being. Bad things.

The group broke up, and as a small band of men wandered off through the brush and out of sight, Sun thought she recognized a few of them—old men, people from her past, faces from when she was a girl, faces from old photographs, people she thought she could recognize from the stories she'd been told as a child. They were all there.

The men faded into the shadows of the night. Even their footsteps seemed to fall away into stillness.

And then Sun heard a cry, loud and clear. It wasn't a human voice but rather the sound of something trying to sound human.

As the small band cleared the rim of the rock, the full scene came into view, and Sun, gripped with fear and dread, had to shield her eyes from the slaughter unfolding in front of her.

It was as if the devil himself had stepped onto the earth and begun to methodically, systematically, process life into the carcasses of expired souls. Sun saw flashes of ancient memory and of memory yet to come, of the tearing of life into vehicles of suffering. Sun felt the welling up of sorrow, of fear, of panic, and of terror as she watched the butchers cleave their way down the line, stopping to admire the sheer suffering of life. It was barbarity, savagery, cruelty, and cold death, all on display for their own pleasure.

And within it all was a low grinding noise, as if a gristmill was crushing wheat into flour. It sounded like the wheel of the old mill, turning, slowly, relentlessly, with the passing of the brook beneath it, which was life.

The sound made Sun shiver, like death itself was passing right through her, taking her with it as it went.

THE DESTRUCTION

S UN'S FEAR TURNED TO anger, and for a moment, it lingered with
her. She pushed it down deep inside of her and then lifted her head.
There, along the tow line leading to the gallows of horses, stood Nellie—
thin, frail, trembling.

Nellie was next.

With that, Sun let loose a scream that made the skies alight with
lightning, thunder, and the brilliance of harsh sunshine. "Whatever it
takes, whatever I must pay, I'll pay. I demand that this end."

Jack's eyes went wide, and he lunged forward to grab her, but it was
too late. Many of the men started after her, ignoring the danger.

She ran faster and faster, until she was almost on top of the butchers.
They howled and hissed and reached for her before she could escape.

At the last possible moment, a massive wall of fire opened up behind
them, and the dark rider, surrounded by rings of flame and hot gas,
overtook Sun and engulfed the butchers. The shockwave of the rider
driving past her almost knocked Sun to the ground and halted the group
behind her in their tracks. His horse flailed wildly across the giant plain
as the rider steered it in and out of the mass of living and dead souls,
engulfing them.

The rider held in the hand of his upraised arm a black skull, with its
mouth agape, its eyes glowing savagely. The object seemed to pull in and
consume the butchers, along with all of the misery and suffering they had
created, and swallowed entire batches of souls that were dangling from
ropes strung up all around the massive butcher pit.

As the rider marauded through the horde of men and beasts, the
far-off red-eyed creatures surrounding the scene began screaming and
scrambling to escape to anywhere. The rider raised the skull high above
his head and then threw it into the distant, writhing mass. The skull
descended on them with frightening speed. A tremendous eruption

of fire and light detonated along the horizon, vaporizing the mass, and sending the remainder of the creatures running and flying away off into the far reaches of the netherworld.

Sun descended on the few remaining butchers in a flurry of anger, the men of the band following right behind her. As she grabbed each of the butchers, their skin blistered and steamed before turning to charred flesh. She fought her way through them, overwhelming them. They screeched like wild animals as they succumbed to her attack. Sun's dress smoked from the heat and the fire. The night sky all around them boiled.

Finally, the fight was over.

The horses that were yet to be cleaved were let down, and as they found their legs, they clustered around Nellie. The men set the rest from the corral free, and the herd itself closed ranks so tightly that Sun had to push her way through it to touch Nellie for herself. She wrapped her arms around Nellie's neck and then stared back toward the dark rim.

The cloaked rider sat on his horse holding the black canvas sack, and soon, a molten shape grew inside of it, expelling light and waves of icy coldness, its glow quickly dwindling away. The rider looked defiantly at Sun and the band of men and then galloped off into the dark in pursuit of the fleeing specters now far, far off in the distance, silhouetted against the remnants of the massive explosion. The rider charged onward, fueled by an insatiable hunger.

Sun watched as the horse blazed a trail into the darkness, and she could see the hooves of the horse flashing in the night—one, two, three hooves.

Loose on the world of men … if the task can be done. The rider smiled.

Great sorrow and relief washed over Sun as she held Nellie and looked upon the dead and bleeding horses. She felt a massive welling up of pain within her for the suffering and loss of life and for the terrible legacy that was this place. The weight of the place pressed in on Sun, nearly crushing the breath out of her.

Nellie exhaled a deep breath of relief but was so weak that she could barely stand. Her wounded leg seemed to be eaten nearly all the way through.

Sun stroked her muzzle and then turned to the men; they sat or laid back on the soil, exhausted, their strength literally dripping off of them into the dirt. And then all Sun could think about was the unborn colt.

In that instant, the men of her band, the horses, and the butcher's ring all disappeared. It was now only Sun, Nellie, and Jack in a place seemingly far away from where they had been. It was a sunny and mild afternoon in a grassy field along a wandering creek. Sun thought she knew the place but couldn't be sure.

Jack knelt by the creek and washed his hands and his face, the grit and the blood from the fight coming off of him in layers

Nellie dipped her head down into the cool stream of water and drank for several minutes. Her raw leg was soothed by the cold. The water seemed to help it mend just a bit, and the frailty of her body slowly resolved. In a few moments, she looked more fit, the way she had many years earlier.

Jack stood along the bank of the creek in the shade of a large willow tree, leaning against its trunk, saying nothing. And Sun stood by Nellie, her skirts lifted up out of the way of the water, and stroked her stomach.

And little Nellie kicked for Sun. Nellie snorted.

"So, is it over?" Sun asked.

"This part of it may be. But there's more to it."

"More?"

"There's more," Jack repeated. "There's another battle left to fight."

With that, Jack turned his head and nodded to a place behind Sun along the edge of the creek. Sun turned and looked and found her breath taken from her body.

There, poised atop his horse, was the dark rider, and his face looked like it was made of stone, chiseled out of solid granite—craggy, angular, extreme, and yet, for the moment, serene. And in his raised fist dangled the canvas sack, with something inside that tore at the bag, as if its contents were struggling to escape.

"To get back, we'll have to get past him."

THE STANDARD

JACK'S WORDS FLOATED IN the air for a moment, and then the entire world went black for Sun, and all that existed was fear. The image of it consumed her, like fire crawling up her spine. She trembled for just an instant.

Nellie called to her, and Sun could see the shape of the unborn colt within her pressing against her stomach, almost bursting.

"There's not a lot of time left," Jack said quietly.

Sun fought herself back into consciousness. She regained her senses and then stood firmly between Nellie and the mounted rider.

The dark rider's horse jostled restlessly in place, and the rider gently restrained it. Sun was instantly struck by how subtle the rider's actions were. He and the horse appeared to be one being.

Sun looked at the man, and her eyes stung. She stepped forward and tried to comprehend his existence and what he wanted. And she looked closely at the horse. It was a massive animal but hard to characterize, as its shape slipped in and out of focus. Sun noticed that one of its hooves was singed.

"More." The man's voice was low, almost obscenely guttural.

Sun looked at him more closely. His eyes were black. The canvas sack he held aloft stank of rotting flesh.

"What is your task here? What have you been sent to do?" Sun spoke, prompted by intuition more than anything else.

"More. To the end." The rider's eyes shifted their gaze, far past Sun, out to an area along the horizon where the brilliant daylight began to dim.

"If I help you to get more, will you allow us to pass back to our place?" Sun asked.

The rider's eyes flared and his voice expanded, engulfing everything around them.

"A deal? A deal? I have a deal. For the shoe. For eternity. In all things."

"Then what do you want?"

"More. Death … I come to end."

Sun was startled. "You wish to end death?"

"I am death. I wish to end."

As Sun stood and considered the uncertainties of this, far behind her, something was happening. At first it felt like an itch along her back, and then it was like someone was blowing cold air across her, the way it felt at night while sleeping and the outside temperature would drop with the windows open. She felt uncomfortable and felt the urge to look behind her, but as she tried to turn, overwhelming fear gripped her.

Jack straightened, and his eyes looked well beyond them to the outer rim. There was something happening.

There was something coming.

A slight breeze kicked up, and as it built, their surroundings started to fall away. The creek Nellie was standing in began to dry up, and the lushness of the spot simply wilted. Sun went to Nellie and coaxed her out of the stream. As she stepped onto the dry land, the stream turned into rock.

Sun lifted her head and looked in the direction of Jack's gaze. Out along the outer rim of the world, a boiling cauldron's worth of eruptions, of explosions, and of massive waves of energy percolated silently.

"The end of death." The rider spoke quietly. "If I am taken, suffering will be eternal. There will be no exit for Man. Life will never succeed. Life will carry the burden of death forever. I am the only relief for Man."

Sun didn't understand. But Jack did.

"Rider, will you show us the way? We have far to go." Jack's voice was steady, but in it was a sound of trepidation. There was an uncertain deal being played out here, and Sun didn't understand it. But she didn't know enough to interfere.

The dark rider nodded and slung his canvas sack over the saddle horn. In its place, he drew out a long battle standard with what looked like human scalps and ears dangling from it. The long, stout pole was covered with scars and gashes, as if it was living flesh. With his other hand, he offered Sun a horse's bridle, which he lifted in her direction. Sun hesitatingly stepped forward and took it from him and then slipped it over Nellie's head and buckled it, taking the reins.

The rider slowly started down a trail away from the creek, followed by Jack, and then Sun, who was leading Nellie along. As they went, Sun could hear the building of a sound, a grinding noise. But this noise was different from before. This noise sounded as if it was reversed. The grinding was now one of building, not destruction. And it crept closer to them.

It was like a giant wheel was turning. It didn't travel to any place; it merely spun on its axle. And it was now turning backward, right over all of existence.

Nellie managed to walk only a few steps at a time, her belly now bulging. Sun could practically hear the unborn foal in its womb, crying to be born.

The scene slowly changed as they went, and in a moment, they were back at the campsite of the band. The men were huddled around the fire, sitting quietly. Some of them were gone, and some of them had regressed back to their sullen, almost grim, appearances. The fire they surrounded flickered and danced, but the flames were cold.

The dark rider sat quietly on his horse, the battle standard pointing high above him. His face was calm, nearly pleasant, but his grip on the long shaft of the standard made his knuckles white, and his fingernails dug into it deeply.

Sun realized that there was no more waiting to be done.

The foal had to be born.

THE BREAKING

S ARA SAT PATIENTLY IN the barn, listening. Nellie was standing, all four of her legs spread wide apart, and her tail was now curled up over her rear, twitching. The young colt was talking to Sara, and what she heard terrified her.

Tom stood by and waited. He'd seen horses give birth in all manner of postures before, but he'd never seen one quite like this.

Nellie looked as if she was built out of solid iron. Her head bobbed back and forth, and then, with a tremor, a massive squirting of birth fluid broke forth, and the entire barn seemed to take on a subtle glow. Nellie squirmed as she stood, and within a few moments, the foal's muzzle, shrouded in its sac, poked through. The young animal's eyes were wide, practically panicked.

Nellie strained again, and Tom rushed forward to help cradle the foal to the floor of the barn. The sac broke free, and the wet little creature lay calmly at its mother's feet, trying to catch its breath. Nellie turned back to see her new offspring, and then turned all the way around, lowered her head to it, and nudged it gently. The foal struggled for an instant to stand but instead stayed lying down, looking around the barn.

Several minutes passed by, and both the animals reached a state of calm.

Sara felt waves of things washing over her, and she wasn't sure it was her own experiences or that of the newborn. She saw light and sound and images of a massive battle going on somewhere out in the beyond. And she saw her mother and Grandpa Jack toiling with decisions and trying to come to grips with ideas well beyond them.

The world of a young girl was now generations away from her. She was now standing, living, in a place where simple life was so alien to her that it felt like ancient memory trying to claw its way to the surface of her mind.

And Sara saw the dark rider and the energy surrounding him—so massive that it blotted out the rest of that world to Sara's eyes. The dark rider … the man … the Horse Man. His mere existence overwhelmed her sense of everything.

Tom helped Nellie clean up the foal, and as he did so, he noticed something.

"Look at this." Tom's voice was practically flat in its tone, but at the same time not entirely sure of itself. Tom's eyes were suddenly wide and angular, like a man who had seen something he had long believed to be impossible.

Sara came closer to the newborn, and her breath jumped into her body in one giant gasp.

The young horse was two-tone, but this was different. She was half white and half black, one side to the other, the two sides battling each other for control. The separation of the two sides were continually encroaching and then retreating atop the crest of her back.

And one hoof, the right rear, was clearly a different color than the rest. It was blood-red, as if it had been dipped in paint up to the ankle.

The horseshoe in Sara's dress pocket began to feel very, very heavy, almost impossible to carry. She continued to hold it secretly within the folds of her dress.

In a single movement, the foal pushed itself up and stood on its own. As it reached its balance, a massive thunderclap struck somewhere near the barn, and the horseshoe in Sara's grip burned her hand.

At that moment, in Sara's mind's eye, she saw the dark rider grinning, like a man who was about to cheat at cards and knew he would get away with it because he knew his opponents weren't good enough at cheating themselves to catch him.

THE MOMENT

S UN STEADIED NELLIE, TRYING to keep her from backing away. The time had come, and there was no denying it. Jack held the reins, and Sun coaxed Nellie slowly to the ground. She struggled but finally lay down on her side.

The dark rider sat nearby, his attention boring into them, watching, waiting. His own mount was hypnotized with interest.

Jack stood beside Nellie and watched the foal come into the world. But as it revealed itself, he staggered back a few steps. The newborn instantly raised itself up and stood defiantly. Sun almost jumped back herself, startled.

The young foal was jet black, with scales and sharpened hooves, and behind its ears and along its back was a small set of what looked like folded wings. The newborn moaned at first and then let loose a ferocious screech, extending its wings and partially rearing up on its hind legs. It was unsteady at first, but as it settled down, it rushed up to Nellie's face and nuzzled itself into her neck and chest. Nellie only snorted and rubbed her face along the neck of the newborn, proud of her new baby, caressing its mane.

The rider sat quietly, his horse shifting its weight from one foot to the next.

Sun realized that she was in a place where her usual understanding of life and existence was completely arbitrary to what she was experiencing. She didn't know whether to be afraid, curious, or pensive. She was, perhaps, experiencing all three sensations at once.

But most importantly, she felt adrift in a world of contradictions, and her memories of her own world seemed miniscule in their dimensions of worth and value. The world was a broken reflection of something now misplaced.

THE WORD

Tillie stood near the sheriff and Old Man Waxman, patiently waiting. All who were there could only wait—and hope.

The sheriff recalled his experience of passing through to this place. He had seen all sorts of scenes from life and experienced all kinds of sensations, from war, from desperate struggle, from broken love, from the Universe of Games. His world now seemed like a vista looking into infinity in every direction. He remembered seeing the scaled horse. It had scared him.

"No reason to fear it. It's less of a demon and more of an angel," Tillie said.

The sheriff simply nodded his head.

Old Man Waxman nodded toward Tillie. "She's right. It's a newborn coming into the world of destruction, prepared to struggle. It wants to survive, and it wants to get home."

The sheriff considered the words.

Waxman smiled. "And it can do things. Some things that can make it better, or worse, for us all. Let's just hope for the best. Nellie's with it. Nellie's got good sense."

"At least Jack is there. He knows." Tillie spoke quietly.

"Jack knows." Waxman sat back in his chair as he spoke. Out of habit, he looked at his pocket watch. It had no numbers and no hands. Here, there was no judging time or the passing of life.

All things here suffered under the same rules of nonexistence.

THE BARGAIN

THE DARK RIDER LIFTED himself off of his saddle and lowered himself down to the ground. The dried scalps and strings of human teeth on the battle standard grated and rattled against each other, and the horse grew annoyed that its rider had dismounted. But the rider calmed the horse with a gentle and, as Sun thought, uncharacteristic brushing of its face with his hand. The horse settled down, and the rider turned his attention to the foal.

As the rider approached the foal, the foal's scales along its back started to grind against themselves, like a viper warning an interloper of impending danger. Its ears went flat on its head, and it bared its teeth, much like a dog. The sound was unnerving. But the rider stepped forward quickly and caressed the young animal along the muzzle and the head, and the grinding turned to the fluttering of feathers. Nellie was quite pleased and snorted and brushed up against the dark rider's cloak, rubbing her face on his back.

The ink-dark scales of the young horse turned red where the rider touched it for just an instant and then quickly resorted to their blackness.

"This is truly the end of time," the rider said. "All things fall at the feet of the young." He admired the horse, and it responded to him by widening its eyes and lifting its head up and down. Then the rider turned to Sun. "I am here on a task. The young one has sent me."

Sun was paralyzed for a minute. "You mean Sara?"

"She has a way, as do you—as do these creatures. They're the last of what is left of light. For my final ride, I am proud to be here."

"What is your task?" Jack asked. He was uneasy with this.

"I already have a bargain." The rider's voice was flat, almost unpleasant.

"What is it?" Sun insisted.

The dark rider hesitated, not wanting to reveal anything. "I cannot speak of it here. This is the world of falseness; all is an illusion. But when I am done, I will be free."

"Free?" Sun asked. "Free to do what? For how long?"

"For eternity. Past life, past death, past existence, and past the stealing of souls. For eternity."

"What do you want from us?" Sun swallowed hard after she spoke the words.

The dark rider only smiled. As he did so, his smile grew wider and wider, until his grin became frighteningly sardonic. Then he began speaking.

"The only thing you have to give is that which I cannot accept—hope, love, empathy, the ability to sleep, all those things that are so much a part of a mortal life. I have no rest to take, only more souls to swallow. Once I am free, I can live as a mortal man, across millions of lives. I can be anyone I have slain, anyone I have scythed down. I will be Mankind. My only sensation is hunger—to feed something that can never be satisfied. It is like fire and pain and hatred. It remains."

He lifted his hand to the foal again, and this time the foal rubbed its face all over him, like a beloved cat might. Then it straightened and began running and jumping, trying to get its new wings to grip the air. The foal let out a playful screech, almost like a crow. It played for a moment, bounding about, and then returned to Nellie's side and lay down with her. The mother and infant cuddled.

"This young angel—it is new to the world, uncorrupted, unobstructed. It can revel in the joy of being itself, for it doesn't know it is the implement of destruction," the dark rider said. "Under a guiding hand, it may discover it is the end of all things, if it chooses to become so. Without such guidance, it merely lives as a young innocent, and it is at risk, just as anything else is, to fall prey to the dark things of the night."

The rider looked beyond Sun toward the horizon, which appeared to be growing closer and closer to them. He surveyed the distance and then remounted his horse. "I have a task to fulfill. You must continue on the path. I shall join you."

The rider charged off into the distance, lifting the battle standard high above his head as smoke and flames trailed behind him. He galloped out of sight beyond the horizon.

Sun stood over the young foal, which instantly rose to greet her. Sun coaxed it toward her and then gently stroked its mane. The young creature made its scales bristle up, responding to Sun's attention. They turned from sharp scales to soft feathers. It purred and then chirped happily.

Jack admired them together but then sensed something coming toward them from behind. He turned and drew his sword just in time to cut down an advancing dark creature, a shadow that had become solid and whole, with flaming eyes and claws made out of pure fire. The foal reared up and roared, baring its teeth and stretching its wings out to their full expanse, and for an instant, it looked more formidable than a demon coming out of the darkest depths of Hell. The creature turned to vapor the moment Jack cut through it, and the attack was over before Sun had realized what was happening.

But more creatures materialized nearby, and the young foal charged at them, slashing and stabbing with its hooves and wings. The demons yelped and ran, but the foal chased them all down and destroyed them, its eyes glaring brightly. When the last one was gone, it let out a ferocious screech. The foal quickly returned to Nellie's side, vigilantly watching in every direction. Nellie trembled, terrified, but the foal only drew closer to her, reassuring her.

"Safe," Sun heard the foal say to Nellie.

The rider's voice rang clear to Sun in her mind: "The tainting of innocence has begun. Guide it with your heart, and it will follow into the light."

Sun took Nellie's reins, and with Jack guarding to the rear, they started down the trail toward the last spot of sunlight along the skyline, the young foal trotting by its mother.

As she led Nellie and the newborn along, Sun realized that she was scared, so scared that she was shaking. She tried to calm herself down, but she realized that her whole world, the real world, was somewhere else. She now existed in a place where death wasn't the end of life; it was becoming a prisoner to dark things that never rested.

And in the darkness, inching closer to them, was a wave of snarling, vicious creatures.

THE TEAPOT

Alva Alicia sat without moving for several moments, her hand poised above the teacup, which she had just swirled. The leaves were confusing, almost contrary to what she knew.

Along the porch of the house, a wispy vapor settled nearby, resting. She raised her gaze for a moment and then, ignoring the vapor, returned her attention to the teacup.

The vapor came forth and hovered in front of her. Finally, she lifted her eyes and stared at it. It wavered for a moment and then drifted slowly into focus. It was a face of an old woman with craggy lines and thinning gray hair. The woman had a toothless smile, but her eyes were brilliant, almost blinding.

Alva Alicia could see that the face was speaking, but there were no words to be heard. The face floated in front of her before dissolving into a stream of smoke and quickly slipping into the spout of the teapot on the table, the china lid rattling and nearly breaking as it flopped about.

The teapot quickly chilled, until it was sweating moisture.

Alva Alicia lifted it off the table, poured more tea into her cup, and then, rather than swirling it, drank it down quickly.

The old face suddenly reappeared in her own, and in that instant, the message of the face became clear.

Alva Alicia quickly went inside.

THE CHOICE

S ARA LED THE YOUNG colt out into the air. Nellie rested nearby, watchful of her new offspring but trusting Sara to watch over her. Tom saw to Nellie, cleaning her up and making sure she didn't have any ruptures or complications.

The newborn looked about, and realizing that it was free to run, slowly began romping and playing as Sara led her about. The foal's two-tone coat glistened as it bucked and tussled with itself, and it let out a high-pitched whinny as it became accustomed to its newfound life. Nellie called back to it, and although it hesitated for a brief moment, it finally ran back into the barn and settled in next to Nellie. It probed her to find the right spot and then started nursing.

Sara wondered for a moment about the dark rider and what he must be doing in the other place. That thought suddenly made her want to touch the horseshoe in her dress pocket, but she resisted.

Tom stepped away from the mother and her offspring and went to stand by Sara, who was transfixed by the strange events.

Sara stepped closer to him, took his hand, and looked up hopefully.

"I miss Mom," Sara said. Her eyes were wet.

"I do too. She'll be back soon. I'm sure. Meanwhile, let's go make a bottle for the newborn. She looks like she's got an appetite." Tom smiled, and Sara smiled back.

The young horse was feeding hungrily, and Nellie seemed to enjoy feeding it.

"Later," Tom said, "you can tell me all about the horseshoe."

Sara's face went blank for a minute, and then she grinned. "Nothing gets past you, Dad."

"That's why I'm the dad."

They walked off to the house, with Nellie and the foal following them to the gate.

Just as Sara was about to pass through the front door into the house, something got her attention. Her head jerked around toward the direction of the tree hollow. She could hear something like a truck, laden with rattling, creaking rubbish, rumbling toward the house. As the noise got closer, it transformed into something like loud bells and then the sound of a dozen voices all talking at once, each conversation nearly indistinguishable from the next. And then there was the sound of animals, some of them screaming, like in a slaughterhouse.

Sara's heart was beating so fast that she thought it was going to burst out of her chest. She fought back the fear, and held the horseshoe tightly in her hand inside her pocket. She wished the noises away, and they stopped.

But on a nearby branch in the yard, the owl appeared, calling to her. With that, she called to her dad and told him where she'd be. Calling for Blue to follow, she scampered past the house, through the woods, and back to the ravine.

Nellie and the foal watched her through the open barn doors, Nellie patiently observing Sara as she disappeared.

The young foal crept closer to Nellie, very much afraid.

The sounds were coming from the hidden garden. Things were about to break through.

THE TRICK

S ARA STOOD IN FRONT of the old trellis. Just as before, as she lifted the horseshoe to it, the vines and branches retreated, until finally a narrow corridor, with brilliant light streaming from it, opened itself to her. Blue settled down in the sandy creek bed and watched as Sara ran though the passageway. It closed behind her and then returned to its overgrown, thorny appearance.

Sara found herself back within the garden maze, but this time it was different. The flowers and plants were much more vibrant, the light was warm and not glaring, and the grass along the pathways through the maze was thick and rich. She felt an overwhelming urge to take off her shoes, but she suppressed it.

After several moments of searching, she found her way back to the clearing where the white stone bench and the arboretum were, and the open-air mausoleum where the many relics collected by the man still rested.

She looked about and noticed a shape coming into focus near her. It was the man, his back to her, tending a budding vine with delicate care.

Without looking at her, he spoke. "I see you. Why have you come?" His voice was more casual, less stern than before.

"I am here to see you again." Sara was hopeful.

"Again? You haven't been here before. We have never spoken before this moment. Why do you come?"

She raised the horseshoe toward him. "We have an agreement."

The man surveyed the horseshoe. "Ah, yes. I had searched for that for many lives. I am glad to see it is in the possession of someone who appreciates its magnificence." The man smiled.

Sara noticed something wrong. The man was the same in his appearance, even in his manner, but she felt a cold sensation creep up her spine.

"You aren't him. Where is he?" she questioned. "Where is the real man?"

"I've been gone a long time; I only just returned here. There's no one else here, and there never has been. When I am here, I am always alone."

"But I was just here, and I spoke to a man. We have a bargain. I have sent him on a task."

The man straightened, and his eyes grew wide. "At what cost? What payment?" The man appeared worried.

Sara raised the horseshoe to him.

He stepped back imperceptibly. "What did you offer him?"

"I offered to set him free for all time, if he completed his task."

The man's face went suddenly white. "There is no one else here. Except, of course—" the man began.

"Who?" Sara was now very afraid.

"The trickster. The shadow. The thing which appears to be but is not. The veil. It is the thing which passes but does not pass through. It is the lurker."

The full weight of what she had done suddenly came into focus for her.

"If you have sent him on an errand, there is no stopping. There is no ending. It will be as all things loose in the world of Man. There is only the end and the beginning. There is only suffering and death."

Sara grew frantic. There was now nowhere to go, no one to turn to. It was a complete failure. The world around her shrunk in on her, and her hands now gripped the horseshoe with white knuckles. The world closed in on her so tightly that it was pressing against her very soul. She was suffocating out of fear.

"But—" the man continued.

The world receded a bit, and Sara struggled to free herself of its grip.

"I offer my service to you." The man looked about, and with a quiet word, the world around Sara expanded and freed her.

"You would help me?" Sara was in tears.

"I am much like you—a child to a world so foreign and so new to me that I cannot see it for what it is. I have been here long before the events of the world, and I will be here long after. My time is my own. I will do for you whatever you need."

"Save my mom and my horse and its newborn. Can you save them?" she pleaded.

"I have ridden into the mouth of evil, and I persist. If I will it, I will see them safely home."

"What must I pay you?" Sara thought for a moment about what she had to offer in exchange for the bargain and was even more scared. There was nothing left.

"I don't work for gain. I exist in the long hall of the Universe, and that which I bring lives with me. I work for the balance of what is. I shall see it done, and I shall see it be right."

Sara laid the horseshoe on the stone bench. "Please, help me."

With that, the man smiled, and Sara saw pure light coming through where his heart and his forehead were. "I am, and I be, so that I may serve you."

The horseshoe turned to liquid and reshaped itself in the form of a circle. The form slowly spread itself out until it had covered the seat of the stone bench, rendering it a shiny silver puddle that reflected light in every direction. The man stepped forward and bade Sara to come and look at her own reflection in what now was a pool of pure light.

She saw herself as a twin, as a young woman, as a mother, and finally as a wise sage. The images smiled back to her. She placed her palm on the bench, and instantly, the images were gone. In their place was the horseshoe, now as it had been. She picked it up and held it tightly.

The man stepped back from Sara, and in an instant, his presence was everywhere, and nowhere, all at once.

The passageway on the other side began to shake, and Sara knew to run for it while she could. The portal became narrower and narrower as she ran. She stepped through into the creek bed as it closed itself, the light streams becoming slimmer and slimmer until darkness overcame the portal.

Sara stood for a moment, relieved that she was back. But then the wave of fear overcame her. She had let something loose into the other world, something that would never sleep, never die, and never grow tired, and it had at its disposal terrible things.

"Sara? Are you okay?" Tom called to her from the top of the ravine, with Nellie and the foal in tow.

Sara spun around, startled, and then ran up the hillside to him and jumped into is arms, crying. Nellie rushed over to her and rubbed her back as she held onto her dad. The young foal screeched and then joined them, playfully pulling at Sara's dress by biting the cloth and yanking on it.

Tom carried Sara back to the house, and by the time they reached the front porch, Sara was asleep, overwhelmed with the terror of things that now roamed free in the night. Tom laid her down on the couch in the tearoom off of the main living room and then went to build a fire in the fireplace.

Nellie and the foal stood outside, waiting patiently for her to awaken. But she would sleep a long time, and she would dream of things and places that, after she would arise, would strike even greater fear into her.

And the trickster was loose in the other world where life and eternity were things to consume at will.

And he was going after Sun.

THE DECEIVER

THE TRAIL WAS LONG and harsh. Even though it was now night, it was hot and dry, and the horses were suffering from thirst. Finally, Jack led them into a narrow gulley and lifted up his hand. The horses stopped, and Sun, who was now feeling completely exhausted, nearly fell to the ground.

Sun was reliving the sensation of when she first made it into this place—the smell of the cold sod and the feeling of the stillness of the air around her. Now the air felt like it weighed a million tons on her, and it was becoming nearly impossible to move.

Nellie and the young foal were trusting in their way of letting Sun lead them along. Nellie helped her young offspring stay with them, and the foal kept Nellie feeling enthusiastic about having been freed from the skinners and spared an eternal death at the hands of butchers.

Sun was now starving for water, her system so depleted she could no longer function. Jack noticed this and came to sit with her.

"Why am I thirsty? This is a place where those sorts of needs don't really exist, isn't it?" Sun's throat was parched.

"The needs are gone, but the longing is even stronger. You're not meant to really be here. You don't belong. You're not going to die, but your mind doesn't know that. It only knows that you should need water. It's something you break when you come here for good."

Just then, Sun felt water droplets on her neck coming from above and behind. She turned and looked up to see a small trickle of water slowly building down the face of the rock wall behind them, growing and growing, until it became a waterfall. A pool formed, and within a few moments, the horses were knee deep in the pool, drinking and relaxing from the heat.

The newborn rolled in the water, looking like a leviathan as it wrestled with itself, finally standing up and letting the water rush down over its scales. Nellie drank again and seemed to regain some of her youthful appearance from before. The noise reminded Sun of the way rain would run down off of the old corrugated roof of the barn, sounding almost like food frying on the stove, slow, patient, persistent.

Sun eased herself into the pool of water, wading up to her knees and finally falling backward into the water. The sensation was odd, like there was nothing really there. It felt just like the campfire she had first seen in this place, it had the appearance of a fire with no heat. Now there was water with no quenching of thirst. She stood up in the pool and was instantly dry.

Sun was distracted by watching the foal jump and splash in the water, and it wasn't until a deep shadow cast itself over them that she looked up. Standing at the very top of the rock face was the dark rider, mounted on his horse. He was nothing but a black figure, sitting quietly, patiently.

Sun felt herself wanting to gasp, but she held her breath. Jack stood, watchful of the figure but equally suspicious.

The figure turned sideways and made his way down from the top of the rock along a path that Sun had failed to see. The rider was next to her in almost no time.

Sun waited to speak. She was unsure of what it might be that he wanted now.

Slowly, the figure left the shadows and made his way into the light, and as he did, Sun realized that it wasn't the same man as before. There was something different about him, his look, his demeanor, even the sensation his presence gave off.

The young foal bounced its way to him, jumping and skipping like a dog, excited to see him. The rider dismounted, and the foal cuddled with him and his horse. They were almost like a family. It was then that Sun noticed that the foal had grown, not just a bit, but dramatically since they had stopped.

"Rider, why have you come?" Sun's voice was guarded, almost reluctant to say anything to him.

He smiled. "I've come to face the mirror. I've come to confront the truth. And I've come to guide you home. I have made a promise to the young girl to see you back safely."

"At what price?" Sun blurted out.

The man only smiled again. "I ask nothing. I am not a mercenary. I do for the rightness of doing. This is my purpose."

"But … but—" Sun was now disoriented and confused.

"The deceiver has already spoken to you? He exists only to consume, never to provide. I will see him soon enough."

"Who is he? Is he your enemy? Do you fight?" Sun asked.

The man only shook his head. "He is a part of all things, a remnant, an afterthought. You know him by many names in the world of Man. He is the left hand. He is ambition. He is disappointment. He is that which casts the long shadow. He is the gift. Everything he will be is tied to those things which defy Mankind."

Just then, a giant fiery ball flew past Sun and exploded on the face of the rock where the waterfall had been. It shattered into a thousand sparks and then reassembled itself into the form of a skull with brilliant eyes and a mouth agape. It flew past Sun back behind her, and as she turned abruptly, she saw the skull fly into the canvas sack being held by an outstretched arm.

The other dark rider had returned.

The two riders surveyed each other slyly, as if they were about to confront each other yet again after an infinity of matches, of duels, of bouts. Neither moved.

"There are no new things," the dark rider said to the other. "This is as it shall always be."

The man standing near Sun only nodded slightly and then thrust forth his hand. In it was the black skull. The other rider reared back violently, nearly bucked off by his mount. His form was now twisted, contorted, almost deformed, and the sack he held exploded into flame.

With that, the two men collided violently with each other so fast that they literally disintegrated, and the moment was shattered by the explosion of opposites converging. There was a rush of wind, a snapping sound, and then nothingness.

Sun found herself for the shortest of moments in a place of nonexistence, and for the briefest amount of time, she was totally unconstrained, her consciousness free of its limitations. The sensation was sheer bliss. And then, another moment later, she felt herself being thrust back together, tightly, like the two polar ends of a magnet becoming a single thing after having resisted each other.

She found herself back at the creek, with Nellie and her foal. Jack was missing, but Sun sensed he would be back. The horses drank, this time filling themselves. And in her mind, she sensed that what had passed before her previously was about to be reenacted. This time, she would ask different questions.

THE SECOND CHANCE

N o one spoke. There was nothing to say. Those gathered near the plantation house simply bided their time.

The scene had been played out over and over again, countless times across the landscape of what had become their existence. Many times the outcome had flipped from one side to the other. Evil had won countless times, as had the powers of light. There were always tragedies, cataclysms, apocalyptic transformations. And there were victories, successes, even births of life. The battle between longevity and the sharp scythe of horrible cruelty turned in an instant. Either suffering or survival prevailed.

Jack found himself standing alongside the wooden fence near the main house's front yard, and the sense of relief he felt was practically visible. His clothing, his appearance, and his sense of self all returned to him. He waited a moment and then strode forward to the house. He passed several others and went directly to Aunt Tillie.

"Jack," she said, more as a courtesy than anything else. They had all been watching; there were no secrets. But she didn't know what he was willing to do.

There were so many things going through his mind—contradictions, assertions, all manner of distractions. He struggled to recover his senses. He chose his words.

"There's no other way." He motioned with his head toward the porch. "It's time."

Tillie considered his point. Others gathered to within earshot to listen.

Jack spoke again. "It's time."

The realization of their predicament was overwhelming to them all. There was no waiting, no hoping. The world didn't peel away its layers that way in this place. Everything was made of firmament. The idea of time didn't mean that anything was passing; it meant a moment locked in certainty was upon them.

Tillie paused. She turned and looked up on the porch and saw the eyes of Old Man Waxman shining back at her. All the other faces looked her way, and a quiet consensus was reached.

This game had been played out again and again, with the tearing down, the building up, with living and death in cycles so massive and so short that existence literally was crushed and rebuilt under its weight every worldly heartbeat. This time would be no different.

Jack stepped through those gathered around him and exchanged nods and quiet words with some of them. He took the steps up the porch to shake hands with Old Man Waxman and to speak to the sheriff.

Tillie met him at the door to the house and handed him a small velvet sack. She stepped back to see him in his entirety before nodding to him and wishing him safe passage.

Then, he was gone.

"I'll miss Jack," said the sheriff. The irony of the sensation of missing someone was obvious to both of them, but Waxman only smiled. He understood.

"Yep, he's a good man," Waxman agreed. "A moral man. Hasn't been a man finer that I've known in a long time."

And with that, the house and the figures there slowly slipped into the shadows of the night, as if they had never been.

THE PLAIN

HE TWO RIDERS FACED each other on a massive hot, dry plain, surveying each other across a vast distance. Behind each was a huge legion, stretching to the very end of the outer rim of that place. They would collide, again and again, and every true horror known to Man would be enacted there, as would every act of bravery, sacrifice, noble truth, and submission. This was a conflict that could never be won, only fought over and over again. It consumed all in its path, devouring entire portions of all things known to exist and regurgitating them to be reborn, reformed, and rematched against one another, only to collide again and again.

The standards of the moment waved in the hot air on the plain, and as the legions marched forth to clash and destroy, a small figure appeared between the two forces. It held in its hand a white dove. And as the forces halted to assess the presence of the figure, the figure let the dove loose, and it flew into the sky.

A bell could be heard tolling, low and cold and with every stroke, the dark forces weakened almost disintegrating, turning in on themselves with quick violence. The forces of the side of the light were emboldened by the sight of the bird flying into the sky and grew stronger.

And with that, the dark legion disappeared. All that remained was its leader, the dark rider, the trickster. He held aloft the canvas sack. Opening it he removed the skull and raised it to the sky. Its eyes were burning, its mouth agape. It clamored to be let loose.

The dark rider reveled in his determination to face down the other legion; his pride, his hubris adorned him, and he was poised to charge forth when suddenly the canvas sack he had carried was snatched from him.

It was Jack.

The skull gyrated wildly, flailing about like a crazed animal. And the ider's horse reared up, toppling the rider from its back, before the nal galloped off into the depths of the plain.

The rider lay on his back, looking up at Jack, and his face became ashen and drawn. Jack held the sack open and commanded the skull to return to it. It screeched and screamed, but Jack commanded it again, and as it returned to the sack, Jack tied it tightly and slung it over his shoulder.

"There is no defeat," the fallen rider said. "There is no end."

Jack smiled. "Today there is."

And with that, Jack drew his saber and, in one motion, slashed at him. The man sat silently for a moment, perhaps believing that the stroke was pointless, but soon the rider realized that something was amiss. And slowly, his head toppled off of his shoulders and struck the hard clay.

The body fell flat to the ground and was instantly turned to dust.

Jack stepped forward and grabbed the top of the rider's head by the hair, which had now turned white and stringy, and lifted it to look into its eyes. The eyes shined for a moment before turning gray and quickly glazing over. The jaw of the head lost its tightness and slowly opened widely. Jack looked closely at it, now a remnant of shadow and a harbinger of things to come, again and again.

Jack took the man's head, and holding it up high, he turned to the remaining legion and called to them. The sound of bells and chimes and gongs resonated throughout them, and the mass of figures slowly thinned until they were completely gone. The plain was suddenly empty, except for Jack and the other rider. The fallen rider's horse roamed nearby.

The other rider nudged his horse forward and approached Jack. He smiled. "So it is this again. The dove hasn't been seen since, well, I don't know. And this time it's you."

Jack frowned. "It was my time, I suppose."

"Was it worth it?" the rider asked, suggesting a price to be paid.

Jack smiled. "It always will be. Even for the smallest soul."

THE GRACE

THE RIDER DISMOUNTED AND approached Jack, holding his hands outstretched. Jack hesitated for a moment and then placed the now dried and shriveled head of the downed rider in his hands. The rider removed his cloak and carefully wrapped the head in it, tying it tightly to be sure it couldn't fall out.

The old canvas sack Jack held shook and began to smoke, and as Jack lowered it to the ground, it burst into flames and reduced itself to a cinder, finally blowing away in the breeze. They stood together on the plain, and Jack was overcome by the suddenness of the change of events. The rider stood by patiently, quietly.

"So it begins." The rider's words were peaceful, yet imposing.

The rider called to the stray horse nearby, which came directly, and he offered the reins to Jack. "It will spare you a long walk."

The sun fell swiftly along the outer rim, turning the sky red, but this wasn't an angry red. It was a soothing, peaceful glow that laid the place into a slumber of relief.

Jack mounted up and rode off, leaving the lone rider behind, shrinking smaller and smaller until he, and the entire place, was gone.

The landscapes changed. Jack grew nearer and nearer to someplace until he was among Sun and Nellie and the offspring. To them, he had just simply reappeared.

Sun rose from the side of the creek and waited for Jack to dismount. His horse stepped into the water and drank for a long time. The young foal watched it as it drank, and just as the great legions had, it slowly faded away into nothing.

"What happened?" Sun asked.

Jack drew in a breath but held it. "A new beginning. You'll be home soon."

And with those words, they found themselves back at the campsite among the old soldiers. This time, the fire was warm, and Sun smelled the camp stove's food. There was no fear, no trepidation. The men and women ate and talked, and some even danced to the sound of a harmonica. They weren't celebrating but rather paying homage to the end of old path and the start of a new one.

Far off in the distance, there was cannon fire and the sound of bugles. The war raged on, and the flashes of rifle fire could be seen, even from atop the outcropping of rock that overhung the campfire. The men kept watch, as was their habit, listening, waiting for an attack, for an ambush. But none came.

Off to the side, Nellie and her foal rested, the men taking note of how different the young horse was and curiously stroking its back and neck. It chattered back to them like a squirrel.

Jack sat off by himself, aware of what had happened and aware of what would have to happen next. But for the moment, he let Sun rest. There was no sleep in this place, but it was nearly like it.

And back at home, Sara had slipped into the barn with a blanket and had curled up alongside the newborn, the two of them sound asleep. Nellie stood by, dozing off. The newborn was now almost totally white in color.

The air was very still, the way it often was just before a thunderclap.

THE PASSAGE

S UN BEGAN HEARING THE wave of monstrous noise approaching from far off. The young foal's ears perked up, and it looked carefully out into the darkness of the outer rim. Something was coming.

It was like a rumbling, as if a massive machine was going out of kilter, wobbling faster and faster, moving toward them. Nellie and the foal were instantly up, and Jack held them from bolting.

"Time to go," one of the men said. The entire camp was up and on foot heading out before Sun could clear her head.

As the noise grew louder, Sun could feel the vibrations underneath her feet, and as it intensified, the group picked up its pace. They retraced their steps back to the knoll where Sun had first entered. Keeping low to the ground, the group split up into smaller bands and faded out of sight. Finally, all that were left huddled around the horses.

Jack slipped the pocket watch out of his vest and pulled out the stem. For that moment, everything stopped, frozen around them.

"Give my best to Tom, and hug Sara for me." Jack's voice was soft and low.

Sun was confused. "What do you mean? You're coming with us, aren't you?" She was shaking.

Jack shook his head. "No. I'm a part of this place now. I have to stay. It's the only way to make sure you can get back. If I come, they'll follow."

Tears were streaming down Sun's face. "No." She was almost out of breath. "No. I'll stay. I want you back with Grandma Sara, the way it was." She was trembling now, almost uncontrollably.

"Sun, you can't stay; it doesn't work like that. I killed the rider. I own his fate. I have to stay. I'm the rider now. You have to go back, or none of this means anything." Jack's face was calm, but then his expression turned dark. "I'm in this. I'll give it everything I have."

Nellie and the foal came close to Jack, nudging him. He stroked the head of the young horse, and it rubbed him back. "You take them with you. On the other side, things will set themselves to right. We did what we needed to do."

"How will you survive? How will you fight?" Sun's voice was breaking.

"I can't fight, not just yet. I'll have to run for a while. It will take some time." He paused. "Time—that's a strange word here. It's not time at all. It's life and existence. Fate is a kind word. Curse may be more like it."

The sensation of the rumbling increased, and Jack handed Sun Nellie's reins.

"Go. *Now.*"

Sun kissed Jack on the cheek and held him tightly. She was suffocating. She could feel him changing as she held him, things beneath his clothes rearranging, becoming tough.

Jack handed her the pocket watch and then stepped back from her.

Sun turned the watch stem backward. There was a whistling noise, the flapping of wings, and the sense that things were literally peeling away from around her; in a moment, Sun found herself and the horses standing in front of the plantation house surrounded by many figures.

The young horse bounded about playfully, free to be gone from that other place and now seeming to be more of a horse and less of a demon. Nellie wandered over to the fence post along the yard and looked toward the trail beyond, hoping to see Jack. But he didn't follow. He couldn't. He was now locked into that world with no way to ever escape.

Old Man Waxman stood up on the porch, and as Sun looked about, her eyes came to him and the sheriff. She was greeted by several faces she knew as she went to the porch, and she felt increasingly calm. This was the place she knew to be home.

Waxman extended his hands to her warmly, and they spoke. Then she went to the sheriff, and they embraced, tears running down each of their faces. The sheriff led her over to introduce her to Aunt Tillie, whom Sun quickly recognized as someone she had seen many times in her life, in various forms and appearances. Tillie and Sun kissed politely. They gently locked arms as Tillie brought Sun into the larger group and introduced her to everyone who was there. Sun knew every single name as it was spoken.

It had been a long line of people, reaching back many, many generations, beyond lifetimes, who were there with her and who had been there all along. They had all played their roles, leading to this moment.

In that instant, Sun realized that everything she was, and all that had been before her, had been building to this. It was a legacy that had spanned dozens of lives and millions of moments, all for this—all to deliver an innocent soul into the world of what may never be.

Finally, the time came for Sun to leave the horses and return home. She bid her farewells as the horses wandered off into the pasture. This was their home now. They sauntered about, enjoying the quiet pasture, and they looked to be perfectly at peace. The young offspring transformed as Sun watched it, becoming more and more like a freshly birthed horse, spry, curious, and devoted to its mother.

The moment came, and she stepped back out to the fence. Turning the watch stem one more time, she simply faded from view. The figures who had stood with her and all those she knew there began to grow almost transparent. Steadily, they were reduced to thin shadows dancing on the ground under the light of the stars.

THE LANDING

THE LIGHT SEEMED TO fade away for Sun, and after a long time, the fabric of her world returned.

Sara was standing there by the fence, waiting, and as Sun slipped back into being, Sara ran to her and leaped into her arms. Sun and Sara hugged and kissed, and Tom joined in. After several minutes, Sara led Sun into the barn to meet the new foal. It came to her side right away, rubbing and nudging her, and then it stepped back and let out a gigantic screech. For a short moment, Sun saw scales and wings on it, just like it had looked in the other place.

Later, after they had all slept, Sara led Sun to the ravine and showed her the trellis in the deep shadows of the creek side. It stood, faded and nearly inconsequential, but it radiated a curious, almost disturbing energy. Sun couldn't move her eyes away from it.

As Sun and Sara walked back through the creek bed to the steep slope back up to the top of the ravine, Sun's eyes strayed over to the old tree hollow, its gnarled trunk and roots intertwined with vines and old limbs. As she looked more closely, the tree itself began to almost change shape in front of her. It looked darker, harsher, as if it harbored something. Sun was unsettled by the sensation but kept it hidden.

There is unfinished business there, Sun thought to herself.

She realized then that something, or someone, would at some point bring her back to that place.

THE EVASION

JACK RODE HARD. He had been riding for what must have been an eternity. The waves of darkness behind him had tried everything to trap him, and somehow, he had escaped them. He had no idea how many had been destroyed as he maneuvered along the plain and in and out of hiding places. The memories of struggling to get home when he was a solider were raw in his mind. The aching, the fear, the unknowingness of every moment—it all was coming back to him in a way he didn't want.

He was learning about this place. It was a harsh, brutal existence, but it was an existence, of some time, at least. He was there, and he could think and feel for himself. Of all the strengths he had, these were the things that would help to keep him driving on.

He could feel the tearing, the ripping, of his mind and his identity. He was becoming less and less of himself and more and more of something resembling the dark rider who had been before him. But he was still himself. He felt a growling in his stomach, an intensity that seemed to latch onto things and draw him ahead, like an unrelenting hunger. He fought the temptation to give in to it, thinking that if he persisted, he might beat it. Secretly, he knew that at some point, he would submit to it, but he didn't know what end would come about after that.

Until then, he would continue on as the man he knew he was. Virtue and morals and a sense of dignity would be the things he would never surrender.

Jack galloped ahead of the dark wave. It was somewhere behind him; he didn't know how far. But he found his actions becoming less and less effective and his options becoming fewer and fewer. Finally, he realized that he was doomed. He could struggle and fight and run, but in this place, time was nothing. Everything lived in eventualities, and everything would come to pass, as it would with his consumption and rebirth in the form of a dark rider.

He was done; he admitted it to himself. But he would persist until then, and the affirmation made him sit taller in the saddle. Jack narrowed his eyes.

Persist.

Jack rode to the cliffs overlooking the farthest reaches of the outer rim, and as he arrived, he realized he was right back where he had been before. This place was shrinking, and it would finally trap him.

He left his mount and began running up the face of the cliffs toward the very edge of the rim. His horse ran off along the cliff face, finally overwhelmed by a wave of dark fog that simply absorbed it. The wave continued on, changing, boiling with souls and terror, raising itself to the level of the highest part of the cliffs. Jack struggled to get there, knowing that it would be of no use but refusing to succumb.

Jack reached the top of the cliffs. He could see over the edge of the outer rim into nothingness. It was the end of all absolutes, the end of the very fabric of awareness. Beyond, there was pure nonexistence, where there was no fabric, no will, nothing.

Staring into that direction, Jack realized that it wasn't a place at all. It was a consignment of nonbeing. To be there was to be lost, gone, and rendered unto the nothingness of an absence of all things.

Jack stood watching the waves of darkness, of glowing eyes ascending to take him. He was caught, trapped, and this would now be his existence. He would become the dark rider, and it would become his legion to be led against all others.

In a final act of refusal, Jack sprinted for the precipice of the high cliffs and launched himself into the open air.

The wave surrounded and enveloped him, tearing at him, and he screamed his last breath. But just as he was about to be ripped apart, something grabbed him and pulled him clear and away. Away to where, he didn't know. He felt the violent flapping of wings and the sharp talons of a beast gripping him by the shoulders, roughly at first and then more gently.

At first, he thought he had been gathered up as a feast but then realized he had been rescued.

He managed to look up and see the young foal cradling him carefully and felt the blazing heat and cold of the outer rim come and go. They were skirting the end of all things, just barely.

The newborn knew where it was going, and Jack suddenly realized that the foal, a creature of this place, could pass between the different realms Jack knew of at will. It had come back to fight.

Jack's skin felt as if it was blistering under the hot sun, his mind was spinning in and out of time, and his ears were deafened by noises so shrill and extreme that he lost all sense of direction. He felt the sensation of being submerged under the surface of a river, seeing the surface and struggling to break his head into the air. With that, he found his bearings He gathered his senses and looked around, seeing only a lush garden with white stone.

He was now within a garden, someplace in between.

Behind him quietly grazed the dark young horse, the newborn, now seeming to be fully grown, its scales and wings looking threatening and wicked. Jack realized that this would be his mount from now on—a soul born of this place, as loyal and lethal as any he could call for. It would be a formidable companion and his greatest weapon.

And in front of him sat Sara, who was holding the horseshoe in her hands. And alongside her, resting on the stone bench, was the gold pocket watch. She saw Jack looking about.

Sara spoke quietly. "He's not here—the other rider—not now. He'll remain out there until you leave. You can't both be here at once. You're safe."

THE REPOSE

JACK'S SENSES FINALLY RETURNED, and as they came back, so did his appearance. He began to look more like himself, and at some point, he breathed a huge sigh of relief.

He looked about. The pedestal where he expected to see the skull of the dark rider was empty. The black horse looked Jack's way and lightly snorted as he yanked his head up and down, teasing Sara, who bobbed her head back at it. The horse settled back down and returned to its grazing.

With that, Jack sat down and tried to take account of where he was and what he had become. For the moment, he was safe, but it was a simple repose. Beyond, he knew, was total destruction. Any secrets he needed to prevail ahead were there too—somewhere.

And his nemesis would know where they were first and how to use them.

But for the moment, he was safe. He felt a deep breath release itself from his chest.

"How are Nellie and her new colt? Are they well?" Jack's voice was broken but strengthening.

"They're fine. The colt wanted to come and see you. It's standing just outside in the creek bed. You wouldn't recognize her. She looks just like a regular horse now."

"And Sun?" Jack's eyes darted about, watching everything around them.

"Mom's fine. She misses you. Dad too."

"I never knew Tom knew about any of this, but I'm glad he does." He eyed the horseshoe. "And that," he continued, gesturing to the horseshoe, "are you keeping it safe?" His voice sounded wary.

"Nellie's new colt will be wearing it as soon as she's big enough. She's almost already grown. I wouldn't want to be someone trying to sneak up on that colt; she's half dragon, Mom says, just like the one on this side. I've seen her change her shape in the middle of the night when she gets startled. … She's big and scary. The crows stay away from her. Meanwhile, I have a new place to keep it hidden. Tillie told me where to put it."

They both admired the horse browsing silently in the garden. "We still don't have a name for her on our side. I thought about naming her after my mom, but it all gets so confusing."

Jack surveyed the girl, feeling a welling of affection for her. "You've become quite the adventurer." He smiled. "You found your way in here. I don't know anyone else who could have done that. You're just like your great-great-grandmother."

"It's in my blood, Grandpa Jack. So when can my mom come to see you here?"

"Anytime. I'm here until I can figure out my next move."

Time. The word hung on Jack's tongue.

Time.

THE START

Sun walked slowly through the woods, not really paying any attention to what was around her. Her mind was transfixed on her time lived on the other side, and she was suddenly excited by the thought that practically anything would be possible there. She had limited herself by her own lack of understanding, and everything that went wrong had happened as a result. She thought about a world where musings could come to life and what she would do in such a place.

Sun was also quite relieved that she wasn't there. The wave of peril and the manifestation of the dark forces surely had conquered the skill of turning intentions into actions. She felt lucky to have survived it.

As she went farther into the woods, she approached the ravine and the creek bed where all of this had happened. As she walked, she felt an odd sensation, a kind of unsettling magnetism that drew her down the ravine and onto the dry creek bed. She stood silently, looking at the trellis where the passageway to the garden was. It stood mute, almost locked in time. But at the same moment, she felt a tugging, a suggestion, coming from behind her, as if something was begging her to turn around.

Sun turned very slowly at first, not afraid but not entirely comfortable either. As she did so, her eyes began to catch something that she knew hadn't been there when she had descended to the creek bed. Her eyes finally grabbed onto the shape, and her heart instantly began beating like a loud drum.

There, astride his horse, was the other rider. His face held a sardonic grin, and dangling high above his raised arm was the disembodied head with burning red eyes swinging by its long hair.

Sun ran up the hill to the top of the ravine and back along the trail leading to the house. It was farther than she had remembered, and as she ran, each step became more and more labored. And behind her, a massive din grew, like the grinding of bones and the crackling of electricity. She ran hard and instinctively tried to keep from turning her head to look over her shoulder. She didn't have to; she knew what was following her.

There, galloping behind her, was the Horse Man, the dark rider, but now it was his own head being held aloft. The head laughed as the rider galloped closer and closer.

Sun struggled to move and finally became frozen in place as the thunderous sounds of the rider approaching grew intolerable, engulfing her.

She managed a final look backward just in time to see the rider draw his arm way back and throw the head, now a burning ball of flame, at her. The heat was intense as it raced toward her, and she felt her body disintegrating.

She heard herself scream, and then she went completely limp.

Sun detected a pushing, almost violently, on her shoulders, and she roused herself awake. It was Tom.

"Sun? Are you okay? You were dreaming."

She cleared her throat and sat up, her hair and bedclothes completely disheveled.

"Yes, I ... uh, yes. I'm okay. Bad dream." She tried to calm down, taking some comfort in the fact that she was home safely in bed.

Just then, Sara knocked on their bedroom door, flung it open and, ran toward the two of them. She was trembling.

"What is it, Sara? You have a bad dream too?" Tom's voice was calm.

She shook her head, slowly at first and then violently as she stared at the window.

Tom looked at her and then rose and pulled aside the curtains.

There, running across the front lawn, was a flaming trail of hoofprints hollowed out and burning like oil pots. They flared and fizzled wildly.

Something or someone had just ridden past the house.

"He's here. On this side." Sara could barely get the words out. "I saw him."

Sun swallowed. "The dark rider. He's here."

PART THREE

THE CRYPT

JACK HAD LOOKED IN every corner of the garden. It was vast in his mind, but as he walked, he felt as if it was merely taking him around and around. He always wound up back at the same place. He found the passageway back out into the other world and the place where Sara had come through to see him. And he had found the spot he called the Temple, which was filled with relics and artifacts from the many lives of the riders before him.

He wasn't tired or sleepy or hungry. He found great personal delight in tending to the plants and flowers of the garden and enjoyed sitting and watching the fountain bubble up water in the middle of the clearing. He discovered the whole experience to be soothing. But he knew that this was all an aberration; he would have to go back out into that place again and do battle—again and again. It was never going to end until someone replaced him.

He was the rider now. There was no going anywhere, because there was nowhere to go, nowhere to be. There was only the conflict of slaughter, consumption, and death by every cruel means and the fight to oppose these things.

The idea of eternity slowly expanded in Jack's mind, and he began to grasp not just the circumstances of his existence but existence itself. There were designs and shapes he could draw in the sand surrounding the pond of the garden that he had never seen before but clearly knew how to draw. There were stacks of old books written in languages he couldn't read but could recite, knowing that what he was saying was verbatim to the texts.

It was as if things were diffusing into him as he spent time in the garden. Deep knowledge—military history, mathematics, languages, art, music, all from different worlds and different cultures—just took root in him and grew. He even spent time contemplating that indefinable corridor between consciousness and the mind. He began imagining the views of other worlds, other places in time, periods long ago, and circumstances long forgotten with no idea whether what he saw was real or fabricated.

And along with this came an emerging understanding, almost a perception, of a much grander scheme, something that extended beyond all things and ruled over them. He tried to characterize it for himself but couldn't quite do so. It was a vastness of great notions and ideas, but it was more than this. It was as if he was seeing the world, his new place, in terms of existence and not life.

The thoughts of this were changing him.

Jack found himself contemplating the genetics of the plants growing in the garden, how they may have crossbred and what further genetic crossing might result in. He discovered that there was a hidden population of insects, silently tending this place between layers of known existence. Bees quietly went about their business, worms softened the soil, hummingbirds spun and chattered as they chased each other between honeysuckle vines, and praying mantises kept the bug population in balance. It all seemed like a harmonious place.

All except for him.

Jack realized that his sense of time, even that which he had brought with him to this place from the world that had been the plantation, had slowly left him. He had no idea how long he'd been there in the garden and no idea if or how time was passing.

And he grew pensive that the moment would come when he would have to flee back into the other place or be confronted by things that had come from there, even things that may have found a way into the garden. He had no real sense of security and no way of knowing where he was in the scheme of things.

Jack was, very literally, adrift on an ocean of time that flowed in every direction, with eddies and currents, massive waves and wind, and silent seas of calm, windless air. He was adrift with nowhere to hope for. The destination was the journey and vice versa. He was where he was.

But the light was always above him, and the light was around him.

The place he was in was enigmatic to him. He began to think very hard about what he needed to do and became lost in the void, which was an endless eternity of missing or changing details. Jack re-experienced the flight from the plains and all the flights before that, and for an instant, he wondered whether being in this place was captivity or freedom.

The thought startled him. This was more than a simple question.

The question grew on him. He wondered where he might turn for answers and if there were any.

There had to be, and there had to be someone who knew them.

Where to go? Is there anywhere else besides here? He pondered this.

How far did that place go? Was there more of it than he had seen? What was beyond it?

Jack stopped himself. Such thinking was pointless. The world, his world, was here, and there was no way out. The only thing to do was to fight. He steadied himself, and his posture took on a more resilient presence.

He pondered the dilemmas of stepping back through the passageway into the place he had fled from. The image of being instantly faced by a legion of dark shadows, of things with red eyes and insatiable appetites for blood and death, which must have made good use of his absence to prepare, sent him into a state of uncertainty. But he fought down the impulse to cower in the garden and raised himself up to a higher place in his mind.

With that, he summoned his mount, which had been resting in the shade of a nearby tree. Now fully grown, it looked like a black angular battlewagon on hooves—huge, thick, impervious to attack, practically invulnerable, with scales and edges like a thousand swords. It happily stepped forward to him, anxious to begin another ride, another flight, anything to experience the thrill of battle and the movement of existence.

Jack slipped on his leather overcoat, donned his large dark cloak, and draped the leather satchel over his shoulder. He topped off his head with his old cavalryman's brimmed hat, which had a black feather tucked into its hat band. And before he mounted, he turned and went into the veranda and found a saddlebag filled with … he didn't know. It simply felt right to take it with him.

He stepped into the stirrup and mounted up, and as he did so, the horse beneath him stretched its wings widely. The breath coming from its nostrils seemed like steam. He took one last look at the garden, the place of no time, and then spurred the horse ahead. It drove forward into the deepest shadows of the wall of vines ahead of them, and in one massive eruption of sound, they passed through and were gone.

THE TWIN

THE RIDER INSTANTLY FOUND himself back in the garden. He was mid-exhale and had been midstride, and for a moment, he had to reorient himself. He had wanted to come back to refresh himself but knew that as long as Jack was present he couldn't come. How much of Man's time had passed he didn't know, or care to know. It wasn't a matter of time. As soon as Jack had left, his will was satisfied. He found himself standing in the garden and felt the weight of the other place leave him.

How many times had he returned here? He couldn't count. How many worlds had passed before his eyes? How many souls had he taken? His eyes belied the words in his heart.

Not enough.

There was nothing like an unsatisfied hunger. There was no repose. It was nothing without the hunt, the chase, the capture, and the consummation. It was all.

The rider no longer knew his own name. He could remember the syllables but couldn't remember in what order they were spoken. He tried to say his name using every combination of them, but none of the words ever seemed to be right. His way of being had given him a new name instead. But he couldn't speak it, just as the other before him could not say it. It was bound up in the laws that ruled this place, this way, this being. It made up what is. There was no breaking it apart.

The rider settled himself, and after setting his possessions back into their places, he contemplated how the garden had changed and searched for clues to what kind of adversary Jack would be. He studied the flowers, the light breeze, and the way the light reflected off the stone bench.

And he considered the absence of the leather satchel, which Jack had taken. There were things inside it that were formidable—for him and for Jack.

With that, the rider quietly made his way through the rows of plants and tended to the young saplings, which appeared to have been nurtured along in his absence.

THE LATE TWILIGHT

Aunt Tillie stood with Waxman and the sheriff on the porch, watching the young horse frolic and dance around its mother in the field beyond the fence. The colt had grown but still seemed youthful in its sense of innocence of the world it was in.

How many colts had been born, and where were they?

Did it matter?

The ironies of this would have perplexed a person living in the place where Sun and Sara were, but here, in this place, there were no trifling intellectual paradoxes. These had all been stripped away. What remained was the purest sense of emptiness.

The cluttering of distraction or intrigue or speculation had been swept away. Being here, if it could be described as that, was like living within a plain house of cards, ever changing with the turning over of a fresh card at every draw. Every turn was a change of direction, and every face card was a weather vane into a different circumstance.

It was a game—drawing, seeing, building to an unknown end. There was no stopping; the game continued—the drawing of cards, the turning over, the realizing that defeat or victory led to yet another game.

Tillie had known this when she was a young, living girl. She had already been connected to this place, this house of shadows. In the living place, there was fear. Fear was real. It was like the grip of the hand of Death—firm, precise, often warm to the touch, sometimes inviting, but always momentary and final. The grip would release, and what followed would overwhelm everything, like the turning of the new card. But here, the veils were gone. Tillie could see both worlds for what they were … a different game of cards.

Waxman stood, his hands resting on the porch railing, watching, listening. The sounds in the distance were like crows gathering. They quietly assembled, patiently watching, occasionally ruffling their feathers and then settling again. Waxman held his gaze along the edge of the outer rim. He could see the barely perceptible low-glowing embers of the edge of creation where the black demons came to life and grew. And he knew somewhere out there a vast legion was building itself into victory. It was the inescapable, inevitable plight that all who inhabited this place accepted.

There was no tolerance of it. Tolerance implied a choice.

Here, it was all that was. Cycles that grew, refined, expanded, escalated, and eventually exceeded their ability to right themselves would finally topple over into oblivion, only to be built again. But the crimes committed against the laws of existence were brutal, naked, and blatant.

This time, it would be at the hands of one of their very own, both to prevail and to succumb—someone from their time, from their memory, and from their world. Jack was now the rider, facing his opposite. All that remained to be known was which role he would play, to destroy or to be destroyed, again and again.

"Jack's learning," Tillie said quietly.

Waxman looked her way, held his gaze there for a moment, and then, wanting to avoid the imposition of staring, he shifted his eyes back to the horizon.

The realization was clear; it was always clear. Jack could survive, learn to resist, fight, even conquer the dark forces in this battle, or perhaps again later, but it would always result in a swing of the pendulum. Jack would eventually fail, and their world, the place they existed in, would be crushed into dust. The dignity of life would be extinguished, would dwell only in fleeting memory in the lower regions, would slowly grow, and would claw its way back into the light to survive and battle again … and again.

"Jack's a good man," Waxman said quietly. "All those years in that hole never changed who he really was. He's the man we need. If he's still a man, he'll find a way."

Tillie nodded silently and then went into the house to sit with the other women. Waxman watched her pass through the doorway, and although he could see inside, he didn't enter.

Tillie and the other ladies politely acknowledged Waxman's gaze in their direction, and he excused himself to wander into the pasture to see the colt. After he left, the ladies closed ranks and talked in hushed tones. Tillie turned down the oil lamp, and the room slowly submerged itself into a deep, warm glow where shadow and light converged.

Waxman knew they were talking, and he knew that he didn't want to hear what they were saying. Even in this place, there was ultimate power being harnessed, directed, and regained. He stayed away.

In front of the women were a teapot and a china teacup. Alva Alicia began pouring tea into the cup and quietly waited for the tea leaves to settle before she looked into it.

THE TIMING

S ARA SAT AT THE piano and watched the arm of the metronome swing from side to side, trying to keep count. Her hands were on the keys, poised there, waiting for the right point in the measure to enter in and finish playing the song. The sound of the arm ticking back and forth seemed loud, almost grotesquely so. She concentrated so hard on it that it seemed to slow, almost stop, before it made its final swing and ticked in time for her to continue playing. She noticed this but kept up with the composition.

Tom watched patiently, following her movements on the piano keys, matching up her playing with the score in front of them, until the final bar of music was played out. Sara finished and then took her hands off of the keyboard. She turned to Tom and smiled.

"You got it. Well done." Tom smiled, and Sara beamed.

"That was fun! But I made a mistake on that second part. My timing was wrong."

"It's all about practice and timing. Timing is what makes the sounds fit, and practice is what makes you make the sounds." Tom nodded toward the piano. "Practice."

Tom rose and went to the kitchen.

Timing, Sara thought. *Timing was everything.*

She looked at the metronome, and even though she wasn't playing, she started it swinging and ticking again. This time, the arm bounced back and forth for several beats and then abruptly slowed down and quickly froze in place.

Sara found herself fooled for a moment, thinking it had failed or was broken, and then she looked beyond the surface of the piano lid to the oil lamp burning nearby and noticed that the flame was bent sideways, unnaturally so, and no longer flickered. The shadows that typically danced along the walls were stopped in place as well.

Sara pressed a single key on the piano, and it struck, but instead of fading, it persisted and held its intensity. The tone was quiet, almost lonely.

"What is this sound?" A voice from behind was soft but penetrating.

Sara recognized it right away. His shadow grew along the wall beyond the piano. It was the dark rider. But she didn't know which one.

"This is music. Do you know of it?" She dared not turn around, and out of the corner of her eye, she looked for her dad. He was gone.

"We are alone." The voice was calm and assured, not aggressive or threatening. "Music. Yes, I know it. I remember it. It's been a very long time since I heard it played like this. I do hear such things, but to me, they are not as … composed." He chose the word almost surgically. "This is more a story than simple sounds. There is knowledge here."

The single note of the piano sustained itself.

"Would you like me to play some more? I can. Anything you like." Sara raised her hands to the keys, waiting to begin.

The dark rider grew silent, almost disturbed. "How did I get to be here? I don't remember coming here. What place is this?" The rider's voice was now a bit unsteady.

Sara looked at the metronome, making a note of the speed it was set on and the position of the arm in its swing.

"This is the real world. My world. This is where we live."

"Live. Live. That is a word which has lost so much meaning for me."

The shadow on the wall grew, its outline distorting from one bizarre shape to another. For an instant, Sara thought she saw wings and horns, but they were gone quickly.

Sara sat silently. Her heart was pounding; her hands were now trembling.

"I have just a few questions for you." The voice was now lower, reverberating. The shadow on the wall grew into a huge, twisted shape, and for an instant, Sara saw the outlines of other creatures struggling to escape from the larger shape. Arms, heads, claws, even horns and tails quietly flailed beneath its surface, like hands pressed against the inside of a balloon, pushing and nearly escaping.

"I … I—" Sara couldn't find her words.

Just then, an ear-shattering screech came from outside through the open window next to the piano. It was Nellie's colt. The shriek sunk into a low rattling, a rumble, mixed with the sound of metal grating against metal. Sara knew this sound. The colt was angry.

The shadow on the wall recoiled and shrunk down to almost nothing. The screech came again. This time, the entire house seemed to shake. And with that, the shadow vanished. The metronome, which had been stopped in time, suddenly began bobbing back and forth and ticking loudly.

The single piano note had disappeared, and now the room was silent, the oil lamp flame flickering as before. Sara's heart was pounding so loudly in her ears that she was sure the house was shaking with each beat.

Sara ran from the piano to the window to see the colt standing beyond the fence, agitated, its entire body bristling with scales and sharp edges. Its wings were fully extended up over its body, and its eyes flamed in the night. It snorted as it saw Sara, bobbed its head up and down violently several times, and then relaxed slowly until its appearance returned to normal. The colt looked about the house and the pasture carefully and, satisfied that the dark rider was gone, trotted back to the far side of the pasture where Nellie was standing.

Tom came through the hallway archway into the sitting room, looking almost pale. "I was out on the rear porch. I don't know how I got there, but I heard a voice in here. You okay?"

Sara nodded quickly.

"And I saw something happen to the colt. It made its way over here to the house in a flash and suddenly looked like a dragon. Did you hear that shriek? That was it. What happened?" Tom looked about the room.

"I'm not sure." Sara's face was pale and blank.

Just then, the phone rang. Tom went into the hallway and answered it. It was Sun. They talked for a moment, and then Tom hung up the phone and returned to the sitting room.

"That was your mother. She's over at the clinic, and she just had a very strange visitor."

Sara looked at the metronome carefully and realized that she may have discovered something very, very important.

THE SWAN

S UN STOOD IN THE garden, overwhelmed by the sheer beauty of the plants, and took notice of the birds that were nesting nearby. The passage into the place had been less disorienting than her passage into that other place, and she had managed to look into the dark walls of the corridor as she had run into the light. She had seen passing images and abstract visions and felt the waves of history run over her body as she walked. The sensation unsettled her.

She looked about the garden and wandered through the rows of plants and stone structures until she came to the same place she had been standing in just a few moments before. She looked in every direction. The place seemed to go on into infinity no matter which direction she looked, but as she walked away, her surroundings transformed back into what it had been before. There really wasn't anywhere else there except what was around her.

Sun looked into the open-air mausoleum and examined the relics there. There were many weapons, pieces of armor, and trophies of war, but there were also groups of objects arranged together—among them old keys, masks, locks, decks of cards, rings, amulets, cups, carved puppets, pocket watches, whistles, bells, and vases. Each was distinctive in its own way, yet similar to the others. And there were books, many of them made of old parchment; some were massive with metal hinges and locks on them. There were also scrolls, hand scythes, and pyramids of every size made from every material she could identify. Some were glass, some were brass, some were gold, and one was silver.

There were looking glasses of all shapes and sizes and hand lenses of all types. Wind chimes. Weathervanes. Hand chisels and mallets. A blacksmith's forge. And horseshoes, many of them. Some of them looked as if they were made of stone, others of china porcelain. One was thin but extremely heavy, making Sun believe it was carved from a meteorite.

But alone, off along the side of the stone patio, on its own marble stand, was a large, red leather-bound book, open to a page covered with what looked like calligraphic shapes and drawings that reminded Sun of cloisonné. The patterns were interwoven, delicate, and as she looked at it, she felt a lifting of her awareness, as if it was growing lighter. She stood closer to it and looked at the pages. The words drifted into different shapes as she watched, as if the language they were written in was changing as she read. The colors of the drawings were intense, and they washed over her mind, like walking through faint water mist from a lawn sprinkler giving birth to a rainbow.

There was a table and a set of chairs, and on the table was a bowl of fruit: grapes, apples, oranges, cherries, plums, and pears. Alongside the bowl were smaller bowls with fresh olives, almonds, acorns, and pecans. And along one side of the table was a hurricane lamp with a metal matchbox.

And there were musical instruments—harps, violins, flutes, drums, even a set of bagpipes. Beside all of these was a set of gongs, one of which looked as if it was made out of solid glass.

Sun surveyed the collection and then turned and walked back to the stone bench, where she sat. The light wasn't warm at all, and it was more of a glow, not coming from anywhere in particular. She looked out past the large weeping willow to a small pond. There were ripples there, as if a duck or swan had just glided by.

She rose and took one more look around and noticed something she hadn't seen before. Hanging alongside the entrance to the mausoleum was a hand mirror, set in solid gold with an ornate handle and engraved back. It was turned with the mirror facing the stone. The gold shone brightly in the light.

With that, Sun turned and quickly walked back into the corridor, which gently closed behind her.

THE ROCKING CHAIR

T
OM QUIETLY ROCKED BACK and forth on the rear porch, watching
the path through the woods. Nellie and the colt stood nearby, the
colt's eyes transfixed on the clearing as well. After a few minutes, Tom
could see Sun and Sara coming down the path toward the house. The
colt grew very excited and bounded toward them, easily jumping the
fence and trotting up to them. Its head bobbed up and down as it rubbed
itself on Sara's shoulder and then dropped into place next to them as they
walked. It nudged Sara as they came closer to the house.

"So was he there?" Tom asked as they got to within earshot.

Sun shook her head but didn't appear disappointed. "No, no one was
there, but I did have a chance to look around."

"Recognize anything?"

"No," Sun said as she straightened Sara's hair as the colt continued to
nuzzle them both, "but I got a good chance to take the place in. I have to
think about it a bit. It's not really a resting place or a retreat. It's almost
more like a cell, a cloister. I can't explain it, but I get the sense that it's
more like a catacomb than a home."

Tom watched Sara with the colt, which she led back through the gate
into the pasture. It ran through the open gate and went back to Nellie.

"So what's next?" Tom asked as he hoisted Sara up onto the porch
rail.

Sun's face turned stern. "I don't know. We'll have to try again. But I
don't want to wait too long. I get the sense from that meeting I had with
the rider at the clinic that he's studying us, looking for something—
maybe looking for a way to find a weakness to use against Jack. I can't be
sure, but he was just as afraid as he was determined to ask me questions.
Maybe there's something there."

"Does he want the horseshoe?" Tom asked, looking at Sara.

"I'm sure he does," Sun answered back, "but there's no way he can find it. And even if he could, he only has one try to get it back there on his own, or else someone has to carry it back for him. Tillie told me that. And neither of us will do that. But we don't want him to find it anyway. It's safe."

"So how do you think all that other stuff got in there?" Sara was curious.

"Don't know, but if we can both go in there, others must have been able to as well. Some of those things look like they're very old, thousands of years. And there were things I didn't recognize, like they were from other worlds. The horseshoe must be just one of the things he needs."

Sara nodded and smiled. "No one's going to find it."

Suddenly, Sara noticed the smell of dinner coming through the front door. With that, they went inside the house and ate dinner while the colt and Nellie grazed outside. Later, Sara practiced her piano lessons, but this time, she left the metronome alone.

THE GATHERING

S UN AND SARA SAT in the waiting room of the palm reader's shop.
Sun distracted herself by looking at all of the memorabilia that was
scattered about the room. It wasn't disorganized, but she couldn't quite
figure out how it had been arranged. There was a system to it that nagged
at her.

Sara was preoccupied with the cat sitting in the windowsill across
the room. The cat blinked at Sara with both eyes at once, and Sara would
blink back. Finally, after a minute, the cat meowed once and then jumped
down onto the rug and walked briskly through the hallway door into the
next room.

A moment later, the eldest woman of the family came out carrying
a tray of teacups and a pot of tea. Sun recognized the fragrance. They
talked.

"This is a difficult thing to do," the elderly woman said. "These kinds
of places are well guarded, and most people with sensitivities to see into
them can't do so regularly." She set the tray down and then sat herself
across the coffee table and turned to Sun. "Tell me again exactly what
he said."

Sun and the woman talked more, but Sara became distracted. She
quietly walked about the room, taking notice of the many photographs,
trinkets, and keepsakes. They all had an old, almost dusty, look to
them, even though they were well maintained and the room itself was
spotless.

Sara tried to listen to the conversation, but she felt a tugging, like
a pull, leading her eyes through the hallway door. She carefully looked
past the partially open door. She could see the tail of the cat, flicking
impatiently down the hall of the next room. Sara could hear people
talking on the other side of the door, but she couldn't see them.

Sara looked back at Sun and the old woman, who appeared to be engrossed in their discussion. So, quietly, Sara slipped through the door into the adjacent room and found herself in another waiting room.

"See? I knew you'd come." It was Alva Alicia, holding a tray of teacups and a teapot. She blinked at Sara with both eyes. "Shall we have some tea? Tea is always nice."

Sara's mouth went dry, and her heart was beating fast.

"No need to worry. They can't hear us. Sit." The woman's tone was soothing, almost peaceful.

Sara sat down. The woman poured some tea into a cup and then, placing a sugar cube and a wedge of lemon alongside it on its saucer, handed it with both hands to Sara. Sara accepted it and then patiently held it in her lap as she waited for the woman to pour herself her own cup.

"Where are you?" Sara asked.

Alva Alicia paused. "That's a very interesting question. Most people would ask 'who are you' or 'what are you,' but you're different. I like that." She smiled, her eyes widening. "I'm here, for the moment, but I'll be back on the other side when we're done talking."

Sara held the cup and saucer on her lap, trying not to shake. "I think I found a way to call the rider into this world without his permission."

The woman paused and held her teacup at midheight before raising it all the way to her lips.

"The rider … he has many names. For the moment, let's call him that. It's easier to pronounce and he won't hear us talking if we don't say his name." She smiled again, and Sara felt the need to say more.

"I want to save Grandpa Jack." Sara's eyes were shining. "He rescued Nellie and her baby, and now he's living in a world he can't escape from. I made a mistake I must fix. How can I do it?"

Alva Alicia stood for a moment and turned her back on Sara, as if she was politely hiding her face to wipe her lips of the tea. When she turned back, her face had changed. It was Tillie.

Sara gasped but instantly felt at ease. "Tillie! I've been wanting to speak with you. How is Grandpa Jack?"

Tillie sat and placed a hand on Sara's knee. "You are such a bright girl. My nephew is right about you." Tillie smiled. "This is a dangerous thing you're suggesting. Are you sure you want to do this?"

"Yes." Sara spoke clearly and firmly, without hesitating.

"You're going to have to delve into things that will appear as paradoxes, mysteries, even things that will make no sense to you. But if you're true in your heart, there will be no confusion. You'll know what to do."

"Who is the rider?" Sara asked.

Tillie's expression dissolved into neutrality. "He's the Watchmaker, the Miller. All which is time is his, because in his world, time is nothing and time is everything. It is the currency of all existence, here and there. You met his reflection first and then him. They are the same thing, fighting with each other for dominance—to have dominion over all that is as it is. You sent him on a task, and before he could fulfill it, Jack subdued him. Now Jack must match himself to something that has no equal."

"Can Grandpa Jack win?" Sara's voice was hopeful.

"He can win, this time or next, but eventually, all things turn. The rider is patient; he has the patience of a million lifetimes across a million realities. There's no escaping him."

"What does he want?"

"Even he doesn't say, or even know. He is part of a mechanism of time. Time is all things—time is life, time is light, time is motion. The passage of time is ageless. Time itself is timeless, if you take my meaning. Without him, what we are would be nothing. There would be no turning. All we know would be consumed into nothingness. He is a caretaker for the passageway from where we are and what we are into the vastness of the brilliant light. There is no passing him by."

Sara didn't understand, and she was confused. She was hearing things that were simply above her gaze.

"How do you stop him?" she questioned.

Tillie considered this for a minute. "There is no stopping him. But there may be ways to distract him. Time is owned by him, but time is vast. Perhaps there's a way to simply slip past him." Tillie held her words for a moment and then continued on.

"Somewhere, there is something to be found—an afterthought, another shadow, another echo. It is there; the rider knows this. It lives on the path that goes in circles. It lives closest to the rider and the farthest away."

Tillie's face slowly began to fade, and within a few moments, Alva Alicia's face returned.

Sara recoiled slightly but kept her place.

"So, shall we have more tea?" Alva Alicia's voice was pleasant and melodious. "Oh, the milk pitcher, it's in the other room. Would you be a dear and go ask to borrow it? I must have some milk for my tea." She lifted the cup to her lips.

Sara set her saucer and cup down on the table and then went into the outer room where Sun and the old woman were sitting.

"There you are. I wondered where you went. Would you like some tea?" The old woman's voice was calm. Sun smiled in Sara's direction.

"Thank you, I have some. May we borrow the milk pitcher?"

The old woman froze momentarily and then slowly set her own cup down on its saucer.

Sara turned back to the room from which she came to see the cat sitting in the middle of the room, watching her. It blinked with both eyes at once.

"Of course. Here you are." The woman lifted the small milk pitcher and gestured toward the other room. Sara took it, smiled, and then went back past the door.

The old woman was distracted but then resettled herself.

"Well, I hope you got what you needed," she said, turning in Sun's direction.

Sun sat still for a moment and wondered what it was she had, in fact, heard. It all seemed confusing now.

Sun called to Sara, who emerged from the back room with the cat in tow. The cat rubbed its tail around Sara's ankle and then walked back to the windowsill and took its place.

The old woman smiled and let them out onto the street.

After Sun and Sara had driven off, the old woman turned to the cat and cast it a stern gaze. She mumbled something imperceptibly, and the cat instantly sat up, staring back at her.

THE SEARCH

S ARA FOUND THE GARDEN empty. She didn't know how much time
she might have to look around the grounds, but she had thought
about what Tillie had said to her. The word *echo* had hung with her. Even
though she couldn't make her way through the logic of the whole thing,
she had a suspicion that maybe since Jack had mentioned that his own
memory was slipping away, maybe the dark rider's memory had as well.
Maybe, just maybe, there was something to be discovered in the garden
that the dark rider had simply forgotten about.

Sara went to the center of the clearing where she had first seen the
trickster, and finding her bearings, she walked directly away from it.
After several minutes of walking, she found herself back at the same
spot. She tried this again, using all possible orientations. Each time, the
result was the same.

After what felt like a long time, Sara grew bored with the circumstance
and decided to give up. She reached down to tighten the laces on one of
her shoes, and after she was done, she took several steps back before she
raised herself up. Just then, she noticed that something had changed. The
light of the garden felt distinctly different to her. It was as if the direction
of the light had moved slightly. She reset herself and this time took a
full stride backward while she kept her eyes looking straight ahead.
This time, the scene shifted right in front of her. There were new details
coming into focus as she stood there watching.

Sara began walking backward away from the stone bench and the
clearing, and after a few moments, she found herself standing alongside
a well-worn path overgrown with long grass and vines. As she pushed the
vines aside, an old grotto entrance revealed itself. It was weather-beaten,
rusted, and practically worn to nothing. She could see the light from
above her streaming into the space beyond the door, which looked like

a dungeon. Inside, as she shielded her eyes from the outside light, she thought she could see a lamp glowing.

The door had a keyhole on its face, and even though it appeared to be very old, it was clearly very sturdy. She pulled on it several times, and it never budged.

So she knocked.

There was an instant change in the sense of air and energy around the door, and in a matter of moments, a small, graying man came to the door. He seemed more weathered than old, Sara thought.

His eyes were hollow and sunken, his skin was pale and dry, and his clothes were falling off of his body. He had an iron collar around his neck connected to a chain that led back into the grotto; the metal had dug away at his skin to such an extent that he was missing an entire layer of tissue on his shoulders and throat.

The man opened his mouth to speak, but no words came out, only dry sounds. He tried to speak for several moments until the word *water* croaked forth.

Sara saw a wooden ladle and a bucket lying in the weeds nearby, and she took it and dipped it into a spring that was bubbling up along the path. She carried it back to the door and carefully lifted a ladleful of water to the bars on the door, which were far enough apart for the ladle to pass through. The man had to stretch his body into an unnatural contortion to reach the ladle. He drank what he could and then rested for a moment before Sara lifted another ladle to his mouth. Finally, after he drank enough, he spoke.

"It's been a long time since I have tasted water or seen another person. Thank you." He managed a gentle smile for a moment.

"Can I help you, sir? Are you hungry?" Sara was genuinely worried for the man.

She grew closer to the door, and her voice softened. "Who are you? Why are you here in this place?" Sara's voice was clear and firm, but she felt deeply confused. She wasn't sure asking any questions would do anything for her search.

The man looked at her carefully.

"Since I was last asked questions, whole eternities have passed, so long that I almost don't remember how to answer them. But I still have some of my own mind left. I'm the Miller. This is my place. I've been imprisoned here for a very long time."

"Have you committed a crime? Why are you a prisoner?" Sara's voice carried with it genuine empathy, and the man noticed this.

The man's appearance changed ever so slightly as Sara looked at him. He asked for more water, and she obliged. As he drank, some of his youthfulness returned. He grew in height, his grayness subsided, and his skin grew smooth and less weathered. His voice improved as well, and his eyes became livelier.

"Many, many lives ago I was imprisoned by way of a trick. I've been living in this hole ever since. I can't die, but I have withered away down to nothing. Everything has been out of balance since then."

He seemed to regain more of his strength, and as he did so, Sara recognized his likeness to the dark rider. He became more and more like the rider, and as he did, Sara began realizing that maybe this was the echo Tillie had mentioned—another rider, another man, an occupant of the garden whom the dark rider had forgotten.

"You look like him—the Horse Man. Do you know him?"

The man smiled. "I should. He's me. Together we were the whole. But he found a way to cut me away and cast me aside, abandon the whole. He's simply a shadow that has grown to live on his own. And all that is, is out of balance. He should be nothing but a fleeting memory. All of existence has been laid to waste by a shadow."

"There was another Horse Man," Sara said. "The one man said the other was his shadow."

The man pondered this. "This cannot be. There is always only me and the echo of my existence. I have always commanded this place." The man concentrated on this thought. "Where is that other now?"

"He was killed by my Great-Grandpa Jack, beheaded. Grandpa Jack has become that rider now. That's what the other Horse Man said had to happen to maintain the balance of the world. It's a duel. He's out there somewhere in that other world, trying to survive."

"Something, then, is amiss—worse than I had suspected."

Sara thought for a moment. "How can I help you? Can I release you? Can you escape from this place?"

The man smiled and nodded. "Perhaps I can help you in return."

With that, Sara went back to the clearing to find a key for the grotto door.

THE TURNING

SARA FOUND THE KEY. It was hung on a wooden peg in the open hall of relics. It was the only key by itself; the rest were arranged on a tabletop in a kind of collection. She took it and then, walking backward, returned to the grotto.

The man saw the key, and his face brightened. "How did you know?"

Sara smiled. "I just did. And I've got other things as well." She pulled her hand from her pocket and revealed the horseshoe. "I have this."

The man recoiled for a moment, as if he had been blinded by a bright light and then slowly relaxed. "That's a very special thing. Keep it hidden from me, especially from the other. It's a tool from another time."

Sara put the horseshoe away and then held up the key.

The man nodded quietly.

Without hesitating, Sara stepped forward, slipped the key into the lock, and turned it counterclockwise until it clicked. With that, she grasped the bars and pulled the door open. It was tremendously heavy, but it slowly glided quietly, effortlessly.

The man reached up to the iron collar on his neck and pulled it apart. The collar fell to the dirt. The sound of the chain hitting the ground was deafening.

The man paused for a moment, surveying the dungeon, and then carefully stepped through the opening onto the path. The light shifted again, now more brilliant than before. Sara saw the horizon grow and lengthen off into the distance and felt a breeze lift itself across the garden. The leaves rustled, and tree branches moved gently. The air of the place grew refreshing. The faint perception that the surroundings were artificial faded away, and a living, breathing place emerged. A hummingbird flew past Sara's face, and a family of small rabbits ran by into the scrub. A praying mantis, green and smart, settled on her dress for a moment before flying off into the hills beyond them. The world had literally come alive.

The man struggled to walk at first; it had been thousands of lifetimes since he had more than just a few feet to stand and walk in. Sara led him back to the garden clearing, where he sat on the stone bench and rekindled his memory.

After a while, the man rose and reseated himself at the table, carving an orange and an apple for himself and drinking something from an old metal goblet. Sara sat with him. As he sat, he transformed. He became youthful, reserved, almost transparent with the lightness of air.

He rose and admired his collections, lifting some things up and holding them. He paid special attention to the weapons and noticed the saddlebag that Jack had taken was missing. He frowned.

Sara waited patiently. Finally, the man turned his attention to her.

"The world must be returned to its rightful way. Your Jack cannot stay here. It must be only me and that which stands beneath my shadow. It must be this way."

"What can I do?" Sara asked.

"What is it you want?"

Sara's face turned itself away, and the man could see she was crying. "I want my Grandpa Jack to go back to his rightful place."

"Then this is what we shall do. There are things that must be done in all places at once—in your world, in my world, and in the place where he is now. But if done right, we may succeed."

"But what about the other?" she asked.

Sara listened to the man explain, and afterward, she lifted herself from the table and ran through the passageway back to the ravine.

The man attended to himself and sorted through the things he needed. He eyed the golden mirror hanging on the wall beside the mausoleum and shuddered, staying away from it. That had been the trap, and he would now use it himself to undo the wrong.

THE SIREN

THE DARK RIDER WAS marshaling his forces to converge on a steep slope of terrain, suspecting that Jack was there. As the first wave of forces moved into position to attack, a massive landslide erupted from above and virtually annihilated the formation. The crushed bodies of the dark creatures melted into puddles of liquid, then turned to dust, and finally swirled back into the air, being lifted back to the outer rim.

Jack had been shrewd. His forces advanced on the now lopsided formation, charging into them, slashing, stabbing, and overwhelming them. The formation crumbled, routed.

The dark rider turned his horse into the wind and galloped off toward the horizon, considering his next plan of action, but abruptly stopped. It was almost as if he had struck an immovable barrier.

The dark rider's shape contorted, barely contained by his skin. His very existence was jarred loose, and the world that he had created under a banner of deceit was now teetering on the brink of nonexistence. He fought to hold his place.

The rider found himself thoughtless, unable to formulate a single idea. He was now like a creature of the outer rim, single-minded yet mindless. Everything he was, and the phantoms of ambition that had grown around him, had been reoriented into the most unnatural shape.

In his mind's eye, he could see a giant hourglass suddenly turn onto its opposite end, and the sand began slowly draining away. And he could see the hand resting on the hourglass, seeming to be patient and strong. The dark rider now frantically searched his mind for a way to escape.

THE CHANGE

S ARA WAS SOUND ASLEEP. The colt was standing by the fence nearest
Sara's window, waiting for her to wake up and look out the window
toward the barn. There was a fire glowing lowly in the fireplace of her
room, and it was completely silent outside.

Sara was dreaming. She could see Jack running for a door through
a burning hallway, the door at the end slowly closing, and a clock above
the door nearly striking midnight. She couldn't see if Jack actually made
it through the door before it closed and the hallway collapsed. The image
made her wake up.

Sara laid there for a moment, thinking. There was something to this
dream.

She slipped out of bed, went to the window, and pulled the curtains
aside to look out. The colt saw the curtains move and straightened its
head to see her. It chirped to her, like a bird, and then rubbed its face
on the wooden rail of the fence. Then it began walking toward the barn,
briskly at first and then breaking into a quiet run, its tail swishing back
and forth like an excited dog.

Sara went back to her bed, and as she did so, she saw light coming
from underneath her door. She could hear the sound of Sun and Tom
talking. It was very late, so she settled back into bed and closed her eyes.

She lay quietly for a several moments and then sat straight up. *There's
something not right about this*, she thought.

Sara looked at the glass of water resting on the small table next to
the bed. She reached out to grasp it and brought it close to her mouth
to take a drink. It didn't taste like anything; it certainly wasn't wet. Sara
set it back down on the table and looked under the door. The light was
steady, as if all the lights were on all over the house.

That wasn't right either.

She looked around the room for Blue; he wasn't there.

Out of the corner of her eye, she noticed that the night outside through the window looked like less than nighttime. It was like a gray glow, not night but not day, and the perception was odd to her. She went to the window to look again and saw the same scene as before. But as she turned away, the room now took a moment to return to its familiar appearance, as if it had been caught in a masquerade.

Sara went to the bedroom door and opened it. A vast landscape reached off into the far distance in front of her. It was a great plain, hot, arid, and dusty, and at the same time, it had fringes that were lush and green.

She looked for a moment before shutting the door and turning back to her bed.

In front of her now was the dark rider, his eyes flaming red. She was instantly petrified, the breath having completely left her body.

"What have you done?" His voice resonated like a huge, clanging bell.

Sara could feel the vibration throughout her entire body, as if she was standing too close to a giant machine. Her first impulse was to run and find the horseshoe, to use to banish the rider back to his place. But as she lifted her feet to run, she stopped and turned back to face the rider.

"Run! I will chase you wherever you go!" The rider's voice was loud, threatening, almost savage.

Sara looked more closely at the rider; he looked to be nearly transparent.

"Run!" the rider screamed.

Sara stepped closer to the rider, and as she did, she felt a hand resting on her shoulder from behind. It was Tillie.

"No, I won't run. This is my house. My world. You will leave it now," Sara demanded.

The rider's expression faded into blankness.

"I said leave. Go now or suffer the consequences." Sara was less and less scared of the rider as she stood her ground.

"I will return." The voice was insistent.

"No, you will never return here. If you do," Sara said pointedly, "I will send you back to someplace from which you will never escape. Leave now."

"No, I—" the voice wavered.

"Leave, or I will feed you to the colt." Sara's voice was firm and certain.

Through the window, Sara could hear the colt snorting angrily. Through the window sash, she could see the red glow of the colt's eyes. The shadow of its shape began to contort into something bigger, more massive, and its wings extended up along its back.

The rider's shape shook about for a moment. The outline of the rider faded and finally disappeared. The hand on Sara's shoulder lifted gently, caressing the back of her head for just an instant, and then disappeared as well.

Sara realized she was still dreaming and struggled to wake up.

She bolted upright in bed and immediately heard the sound of crickets outside, and up the hollow, she could hear the frogs in the pond. There was no light coming from under the door, and Blue sat up from his pillow to look at her.

She quickly went to the window to see the colt, which was grazing on grass several yards beyond the fence. It lifted its head and looked her direction, its ears flicking back and forth, and then went back to his foraging.

Sara relaxed. Blue lowered his head back onto his pillow and let out a light huff of air.

She turned toward the bed and caught a glimpse of something in the corner of the room. It was Tillie. Sara was startled, but she smiled and stepped forward toward her. Tillie smiled back and then slowly faded from view.

THE RETURN

THE MAN REMAINED AT the table, watching the birds and the wisps of dandelions drifting past him on the light breeze. In front of him was a small collection of items, taken from among the groups of things arranged all around the open-air mausoleum.

The man paused for a moment, and in his mind's eye, he could see Jack leading a charge against a dark wave of things that had been spawned out of the dark matter of the outer rim. Jack was slowly losing his identity to the role he thought he should be playing.

The time left to intervene was growing short.

The man assembled his items, donned his own heavy cloak, and hoisted his bag up over his head onto his shoulder. Before he left the garden, he took a peach from the fruit bowl on the table and carefully wrapped it in a cloth napkin, which he gently slipped into the bag.

The plan now was to find Jack and help him avoid another armed confrontation with the trickster. There was more than the simple act of perishing at risk; there was the entire mechanism of time and existence at stake.

He would first have to convince Jack that he himself was not the trickster and then further convince him to help with the plan. Sara came to mind for a fleeting moment, as did Sun and the colt.

As the man stepped past the wall near the table, he carefully, carefully, turned the golden framed mirror around, avoiding looking into the mirror himself and covering his eyes as he stepped away from it.

That had been the trap before. This time, it would be the trap for something else.

THE MOON

J ACK SAT QUIETLY IN the crevice high above the plains. The hot air was
oppressive, but he waited until the glow on the far horizon increased
in intensity, just a bit. It meant that souls were being eaten and destroyed
out along the fringe of existence. The light slipped away from the land,
and a ghostly glow grew in the sky. It was like eternal twilight.

The sun was gone, but the heat remained. He struggled to forget the
need to drink. There was no quenching of thirst, and water didn't exist
here, only shadows of memories. He remembered drinking that bucket
of fresh water at the shack when he was running for his life, still alive. It
now felt like it had been a million years ago. He resisted thinking about
water or food or sleep. There were none of these things here; they simply
didn't exist.

Jack's attention was focused on the outer rim, but the sound of some
rocks slipping caught his ear. He prepared himself and then sprang out
of the crevice with his saber in his hand. A figure was standing uphill
from him, just far off enough to be nondescript. It was a tall, thin figure,
wrapped in darkness. It didn't advance, didn't retreat. It stood still.

Jack considered the situation. There was no reason to run and no
reason to fight, so he sheathed his saber and, mindful of the surroundings,
approached the shape. Jack lifted a hand toward his mount, which had
begun to rear itself up and extend its wings. The horse backed down a
bit but kept an eye on the shape.

As Jack got closer, he could see the face. It was not the rider, but it
was like the rider. He sensed that something important had come about.
In his mind, he saw the image of an hourglass draining of its sand and a
dimly light hallway with a door slowly closing.

"I see you," the man said quietly. "Perhaps we can go up to the cave
above the ridgeline. We'll be protected there from the heat."

"Why would you be concerned about my comfort?" Jack asked.

The man loosened his wrap and let the folds of cloth fall about him. "Because here, I too am an opponent." The man nodded toward the higher part of the ridge. "Come with me; we have much to discuss."

Again, Jack surveyed his surroundings and then made a gentle clicking noise with his tongue. His mount materialized from the shadows where it had been lurking. The man turned the horse's direction and clicked his tongue as well, but in a slightly different cadence, and the horse stepped forward willingly.

Jack followed the figure up the moraine, where the figure pointed out a slight edge in the rock face. "There." The man hiked even higher up the slope and stepped toward it, and turning himself sideways, he slipped through it. The horse stood for a moment and then turned itself around and looked out across the terrain before finally carefully lying down and making itself as small as possible against the rocks.

Jack followed, barely squeezing through the narrow fissure. When he got inside, the oppressive heat of the plains was gone, and it was actually chilly. There was already a small fire burning in a rock fire pit, adding light to the walls of the cave. The figure had disrobed and relieved himself of his satchel and was now sitting on a rock nearby.

Jack looked about the cave. It was clear to him that this had been a place used for shelter and retreat many times before. He would have never found it on his own.

"So, we are here." The man's voice was low and quiet. "It's quite cool inside, as you go deeper. We're close to the boundary between this world and the next."

Jack nodded carefully. He looked past the man down into the maw of the dark cavern and could see, faintly, something looking like a whirlpool of air and dust and light. It was as if the very fabric of matter and time were being crushed in a crucible.

The man nodded. "Down there, existence is mixed into creation. Time, life, destiny—all of it becomes real. You can go there if you choose. There are an endless number of possibilities for you. But once you go, you can never return to this place or the reality of your memories. You will become something in some other corner of time. Perhaps our own company will suffice for the moment?"

244

Jack frowned. "I'd enjoy the company more if you'd tell me who you are or, perhaps more importantly, why you're here. There shouldn't be any like you, except, of course, for the other."

"This is true. The other isn't who he's portraying himself to be. I've come to correct this."

Jack considered this. He didn't have an opinion one way or another until after several moments had passed, and then the logic of the situation seemed to creep into him.

"As for you," the man continued, "you shouldn't be here either. This is not your place, not your role. I intend to correct this as well."

Jack discreetly slipped his hand off of his lap toward the hilt of his saber, but the man motioned him to stop.

"That's not necessary. I can only succeed at these things by seeing you safely back to where you belong. Any other change would only make things much more complicated."

"The other, the one still here, he volunteered to correct things too," Jack noted. "And the one before him took a bargain to do the same thing. How do I know—"

The man reluctantly shook his head. "Always the same—deception, lies, hollow words. He's the part that doesn't breathe. There is no bartering here, no retaining of services. Those are from the minds of Men. I do as I choose. I create the consequences. I am the solution."

"So what do you want?" Jack finally asked. "I have no choices here in this place. I can fight to survive, or I can be consumed forever. Losing isn't a choice."

The man carefully reached into his bag, removed the cloth wrapping, and unfolded it.

In his hand was the peach.

Jack instantly knew what it meant. It was the one thing that no one could have stolen from his mind or fabricated. He nodded. "Tell me what you want to do."

The man took a long twig and began drawing shapes in the dirt, and Jack drew closer to listen.

THE BAIT

S ARA SAT AT THE piano. She played as before, patiently keeping up with the metronome. And at the precise moment she felt the urge, she held her single note and watched the arm of the metronome slowly decelerate until it was completely frozen. Everything in the room was locked in time. She could see the eyes of the colt looking at her through the open window.

Just as before, a shadow grew onto the wall. The dark rider had returned.

Sara held her breath.

"So, you have found a way to call me into this world. Good, I will enjoy laying it to waste, as I have all the other worlds. You don't know what you've done. I'll—" The rider's voice stopped abruptly.

Next to Sara on the piano bench was a horseshoe, and it was beyond her attention. She was focused on the piano and had left it recklessly unguarded.

Without saying a word, he lunged for it and took it. He fled the room, passing right through the wall into the pasture and up the path toward the ravine. The colt turned to solid flame and roared as the rider ran past it. The rider ran, leaving his mount behind in the field near the barn. As soon as he was out of sight, the colt settled back down and wandered over to the horse and, with a nudge, led it into the barn where there was food.

THE PLOY

T OM STOOD BY THE fence post with the whistle. He didn't feel frozen in time, but he waited for Sara to rise from the piano and move to the window. As soon as he saw her, he raised the whistle to his lips and blew the whistle once.

One long breath's worth of air, and it was done.

The rider, still running quickly, neared the old trellis, and as he held the horseshoe up, the passageway opened. He rushed in. But somewhere within the corridor, as he rushed toward the garden, something passed him going the other direction. Before he could gather his senses and identify the escapee, he was already into the garden, and the passageway had closed behind him. Whatever it was had fled.

Tom waited at the fence post, and within a moment, a gray wisp of a shadow grew in front of him.

It was Jack. Tom had called him back.

Jack found his shape, and when he was finally all present, he smiled. He and Tom embraced as best as they could.

Jack was free.

Sara went back to the piano and sat, pressing the single key. The long sustained note slowly faded away. The metronome swung back into cadence, and the world resumed.

THE HOMECOMING

Jack and Sun materialized in front of the plantation house, and Sun instantly noticed that things were different. It was a bright, sunny day. The clouds looked as if they'd been brushed overhead by a painter as they swiftly moved across the sky, but there was no real wind to push them, only a very light breeze. The trees were green, the smell of the flowers was almost intoxicating, and the sensation of being free of fear and trepidation was as if all of the burdens of life had simply vanished. Sun felt so relieved that she nearly collapsed into the grass.

There, along the fence, were all of the faces she had met and seen and known, and as Jack stepped forward, the group of people surrounded him and congratulated him. He made his way through the throng of people, finally coming to Tillie and the sheriff. The three of them embraced, and Jack handed back the small bundle he had taken from Tillie before. She nodded and went up the stairs into the house, returning it to its place.

Jack finally made it up to the porch where Old Man Waxman was standing proudly. They shook hands and finally gently embraced each other in a gentlemanly way, Waxman smiling broadly, and then joined hands in a double handshake.

Jack and Waxman turned back toward the front door of the house to find Tillie standing there and with her was Alva Alicia. She had dark, brooding eyes, and yet she was hauntingly beautiful. She seemed almost ageless, but formidable.

Alva Alicia's eyes were tense at first, but quickly relaxed. "So, we are whole." She looked at Jack carefully, checking his eyes. "You are whole as well, and you are free, as are we all. The trial is done." She gently nodded to him, and he returned the gesture.

Just then, Grandma Sara rushed up the stairs in an uncharacteristic hurry. Jack saw her and met her on the top stair, and they embraced tightly.

Sun was so overwhelmed with emotion that she could hardly move. The world, her life, and the entire history of her family had been set to right. The welling up of tears of joy overcame her, and as she felt a single teardrop fall from her eye, the entire group of people turned to her and bid her thank you.

She looked at every single face, and as she did, she committed each to memory. When she was finally done, she felt compelled to bow slightly toward them all, and the warmth of the sun above her filled her to the brim of sensation. She was totally, completely whole.

Sun looked at the gold pocket watch in her hand. It was time to go home. She looked back to the crowd of people and smiled. She pulled out the watch stem and carefully turned it backward and sent herself to her own time.

With that, they all began fading from view, and in a moment, she found herself back at her own home. Sara ran down the stairs to her and jumped into Sun's arms.

THE DEFILING

T HE MAN STOOD SILENTLY. In front of him, the dark rider had materialized in the garden and, realizing that he had been trapped, had struggled wildly in place as if bound by ropes. The trickster was beyond logic now; there was no escaping his plight, and his destiny was now to slip into the grotto to perish amid all the other lost dreams of the world.

The trickster had been caught.

The man looked upon the dark rider with no more compassion or interest than a person seeing a pile of leaves burning in the late autumn evening. The fire would burn, the pile would diminish, and finally a spot would remain where the memory of the pile might exist for a moment. Afterward, the thought would be gone, and any recollection of it would be fleeting.

"Your time is no more," the man said.

"Time … my time … I don't know what that means." The dark rider smiled. "I exist no matter if or what time is."

"You'll have plenty of lives to consider this. This is done, and you are no more." With those words, the man raised the mirror to the face of the dark rider, who was instantly consumed by the image he saw and was dragged into it, like a dust devil flittering in the afternoon wind. In a moment, he was gone.

The man raised the mirror above his head and in one motion cast it down onto the marble stone beneath his feet. The mirror shattered; the frame tumbled around and then lay still.

Off in the distance, the man could hear the prisoner shouting through the bars of the door of the grotto, but the noise was eventually absorbed by the sounds of nature and wind in the garden. The vines and brush quickly overgrew the doorway, and within a moment, the grotto was gone. All that remained was a thicket alongside a pathway leading out to the pond beyond the garden.

The man settled into his place, taking account of all the things that had happened and all the things that should have been attended to during his long imprisonment.

He had much work to do and many battles to fight. He looked at his mount grazing nearby, the now fully grown foal, which looked as if it was made of millions of daggers of sharp metal and black iron. It had grown to the size of a dragon. Its eyes glowed red-hot and then subsided.

He smiled. All of time was again his.

THE PASSING

S ARA CAME TO THE table and sat beside the man. They remained silent for a long time. Finally, the man rose, took his violin from the mausoleum, and played a haunting melody. Sara couldn't identify it, but it sounded almost too familiar to her. Sara went to the harpsichord and found that she knew the melody. They played together, the man quite impressed.

"I didn't think I knew that song," Sara admitted.

"There are many pleasant things you will discover you know. It's only a matter of time." The man grinned. "Time."

Finally, Sara lifted herself from the chair and walked to the center of the garden by the stone bench. She looked around and then turned toward the man.

She started to say thank you, but the man stopped her gently with a raised hand.

"Instead, shall we simply say until we meet again?" The man grinned wryly, but Sara detected something in his expression.

She would see him again. He would see to it.

Sara nodded and looked beyond the man into the pasture where she could see the winged colt grazing. It was now a massive beast, its coat and mane looking like razor-sharp black glass, its hooves glowing like fire, and its wings wickedly angular. The horse saw her and instantly settled its coat and wings down and jerked its head at her. Then it resumed its grazing. Its eyes went dark and seemed to radiate like diamonds.

"Yes, the mount. He's as powerful as he is wise. He will be a formidable companion," the man noted.

Sara smiled and nodded politely. Then she turned and strode quickly back through the corridor and into the passageway leading out to the ravine. The colt on her side stood there, waiting for her to come out. As she exited, the thicket corridor began to collapse in on itself, as if in all finality the passageway was now closed for good. She looked down the creek bed and noticed the old tree hollow that had always disturbed her was now green and spry, and leaves were sprouting from its limbs.

Sara took a last look around and then slipped her arm around the neck of the young horse. They both climbed back up to the top of the ravine, where Nellie and Blue stood patiently.

Sara reached into her pocket out of habit, searching for the feel of the horseshoe, but then realized it was gone. It now existed where it ought to be. There were no more charms to be used ... until, of course, the discovery of the next talisman, which hung on a chain, innocently, quietly, from an old crystal glass doorknob.

Sara could see it in her mind. Its time would come.

Time.

Time *indeed*.

Royce Walker can be reached at shadow-whistler@earthlink.net

The Shadow Whistler PGP Public Key can be downloaded from the PGP Key Server at ldap://keyserver.pgp.com

PGP Fingerprint:
6B91 AFC5 6033 EF7F 5D84 F0CB 2C2C 14D1 0EE1 223E

-----BEGIN PGP PUBLIC KEY BLOCK-----
Version: PGP 8.1

mQGiBFKnozURBADL5sKcsSyCfYccWM40jcK98usK57EEigP8DLtTQDJNLbn2bsUa
dCeO9IoZA3rHn9ghRIC84wI+QP2VtLKEXK98epAjmbpGqTMiCg3mmCYMgWHuUBDM
PCgqaWqF8+WrP/s5tVDydWtN/3RAi862W+rN28EOGuLMeS/htCRvo97jmwCg/5gL
LlZf8ci0Ga7L9SixsxO49ZcD/37ICq10ariHX8HmE9dzYnQs3wi05mx3qIPXuIq6
5m17f33jyNs2I9F/tW2CncJf6WyKEOn7F8sOgtJq31ofXcDVO0dWIECZ6uTe+4Dc
nRagrc5Yxaf23BhC3nXX87MoKozegHzq6tf5ZhcJ+X/g0PfyIPRHInDtvybh5yAp
ASuYBACeRqytwmwfqg/Nl+ZAx5UWu4zf88kOcPkQrm651FhgCyplSwabWsmpMol5
e8777fZLoDNIgA/QjlKIu6gqpSbxnCT+7ddgDdqAn6Czq8mIc0eL0paaMi/gQTIr
orFuYr2o68HjeIQDGGfnUsYyeJiZKn39eJPuNoRKz2XQ2zhW/rQvU2hhZG93IFdo
aXN0bGVyIDxzaGVkb3ctwhpc3RsZXJAYXZZWFydGhsaW5rLm5ldD6JAF0EEBECAB0F
AlKnozUHCwkIBwMCCgIZAQUbAwAAAAUeAQAAAAAKCRAsLBTRDuEiPnEOAKDwRUSO
6JsoeejgzH5NZxG4vhzrWQCgmtQh+KVqiW5xG2EETu+6ubvLLrC5BA0EUqejNRAQ
APKkYoH5aBmF6Q5CV3AVsh4bsYezNRR8O2OCjecbJ3HoLrOQ/40aUtjBKU9d8AhZI
gLUV5SmZqZ8HdNP/46HFliBOmGW42A3uEF2rthccUdhQyiJXQym+lehWKzh4XAvb
+ExN1eOqRsz7zhfoKp0UYeOEqU/Rg4Soebbvj6dDRgjGzB13VyQ4SuLE8OiOE2eX
TpITYfbb6yUOF/32mPfIfHmwch04dfv2wXPEgxEmK0Ngw+Po1gr9oSgmC66prrNl
D6IAUwGgfNaroxIe+g8qzh90hE/K8xfzpEDp19J3tkItAjbBJstoXp18mAkKjX4t
7eRdefXUkk+bGI78KqdLfDL2Qle3CH8IF3KiutapQvMF6PlTETlPtvFuuUs4INoB
p1ajFOmPQFXz0AfGy0OplK33TGSGSfgMg71l6RfUodNQ+PVZX9x2Uk89PY3bzpnh
V5JZzf24rnRPxfx2vIPFRzBhznzJZv8V+bv9kV7HAarTW56NoKVyOtQa8L9GAFgr
5fSI/VhOSDvNILSd5JEHNmszbDgNRR0PfIizHHxbLY7288kjwEPwpVsYjY67VYy4
XTjTNP18F1dDox0YbN4zISy1Kv884bEpQBgRjXyEpwpy1obEAxnIByl6ypUM2Zaf
q9AKUJsCRtMIPWakXUGfnHy9iUsiGSa6q6Jew1XrPdYXAAICEACVtWC/yVZvVUSC
bmg05660pW8xX6UoenHmArwe+ss84erP36KTVOG0LUziMjNRYtRomeoIgLWJMrll
rRkyELkEjJOdLpUb+KW8+GVFmas75s4qcE4n7ooDBoCfsUf2Dgaup8cg3xurpf4R
D/NuX40VwsCEqbKwK4lT6o+o8+UO5evvsoDd4TeFsTbCCb0wPjitLzsJ7gVeDdl6
Foy3xH0Mb5fuRHuHb+24AGwCyBzJ1uuEdtDu/Qkfe3yG5DysXIUZ88YLJfWhDCyb
5dtJptWs0/PChUHwUegTpSZbIiKiI2dIAk91/5Q8RvHeXj6apfeRlcUV00XtryZb
UTguanryAVRSIVTmWpXCiERsDYGu3fWDGSAEjM6ULljGF7cH1dfZYQl3W7WujeB5
iHQvrTYzPo2hnnodkWvoiAfwdKW57M+gOZw0qJuXQ0V2nNDnwCC0Vl/ubihnoh7R
QwRINq7rBl/SjM/OIIjiHXV7qfVcMpf6CE/hbLTltQ52JWppCu18OPYJixaMZjcK
qB4up5yTO7evV2Q8As+JLyBgqAEWjTkQv8jbP59F0QLOIaF/gJySA/iIWRWjH4n2
e0CTGzZjmBLALhI1HbkoW0CKZS30AoEWXAxSfTC1wQwQ/EUOMwnZIITBGVI9qFIN
+pS02GwaqnC3OSrZSDhT9tKursqE5YkATAQYEQIADAUCUqejNQUbDAAAAAAKCRAs
LBTRDuEiPmyBAJ456xHexo6ExneFT78tdsaMSjuqNQCfScJIbYUh27Bk1dOKYCcA
+5Tc2j+5BA0EUtSU3BAQAPKkYoH5aBmF6Q5CV3AVsh4bsYezNRR8O2OCjecbJ3HoL
rOQ/40aUtjBKU9d8AhZIgLUV5SmZqZ8HdNP/46HFliBOmGW42A3uEF2rthccUdhQ
yiJXQym+lehWKzh4XAvb+ExN1eOqRsz7zhfoKp0UYeOEqU/Rg4Soebbvj6dDRgjG
zB13VyQ4SuLE8OiOE2eXTpITYfbb6yUOF/32mPfIfHmwch04dfv2wXPEgxEmK0Ng
w+Po1gr9oSgmC66prrNlD6IAUwGgfNaroxIe+g8qzh90hE/K8xfzpEDp19J3tkIt
AjbBJstoXp18mAkKjX4t7eRdefXUkk+bGI78KqdLfDL2Qle3CH8IF3KiutapQvMF
6PlTETlPtvFuuUs4INoBp1ajFOmPQFXz0AfGy0OplK33TGSGSfgMg71l6RfUodNQ
+PVZX9x2Uk89PY3bzpnhV5JZzf24rnRPxfx2vIPFRzBhznzJZv8V+bv9kV7HAarT
W56NoKVyOtQa8L9GAFgr5fSI/VhOSDvNILSd5JEHNmszbDgNRR0PfIizHHxbLY72
88kjwEPwpVsYjY67VYy4XTjTNP18F1dDox0YbN4zISy1Kv884bEpQBgRjXyEpwpy
1obEAxnIByl6ypUM2Zafq9AKUJsCRtMIPWakXUGfnHy9iUsiGSa6q6Jew1XrPdYX
AAICD/4lcUepCReu1EEJZlTe9Nqxf5j1cYBpJoyPTYCOIAtjjTFcqJB4c8ScTt+S
12GZ/wkQJQi+9wGCoTaA8IOwXCn2jkmaj0ZayxAEQBuOpeyosh6V4xv3VpPM4I4n
1rQ6fiFOc2XH1PxjcBXubC6ABRiTql7mC02+RlHgjau43UBqtf/qSujD0aSVT3s/
1azqSTjZjeV7Zv4VmyRPht9kWg3w1MgV3kAgLzS+N/2NZar8M8holgWbHRJLqnJV
LtuN3pD2BBbZVATr2p7tySc/3K6/H417kU/Qix3PbETgV2DFkbTdg94BNLc49kaH
xBQ5+Xul/Xm61JimeHCvWI9NbE/7dxWv002Y0LP+CfEQE4EB+TQoEYKbRwZAYCJC
h09+k4hjwWr1xGk9yzEsMxkKlnMLQhUIVHSnUc2pHBy/xlDPWbVVwYeU8Qayeycs
SzLCoPSv7VLjCulk0Q/CvCjuoLNgplK3PXzZOt8YARau5+sdn2vpkgDnOrJlVPzG
fgNP/KeYVSwpy48S6sCPRuNZmMc6qTG5x7J5Cnqr4N+wO/cXzX4C6e0nWWBJrRkY
4u5zReoj7yoxBwytvZtlF50hrq0bYv25ixV7VWiChL7tSDclLWSrwf4r+e4fD+5L
/ENYSGjyqf2f3GlCQKV0lbK93gQ2InDJefXN7Sm8QuIVPXrjGokATAQYEQIADAUC
UtSU+wUbDAAAAAAKCRAsLBTRDuEiPsbcAJ91ITggx2BlXt0U2Zvr4BtKtUX7PACg
v882ELnQSOvOXTHnSU5gZNomeOI==Sk7P

-----END PGP PUBLIC KEY BLOCK-----